M000187941

Praise for The Darkness . . .

"The Darkness is a powerful and edgy story about a serial killer's search for his soul. A dynamite premise! With its stunning plot and razor-sharp writing, The Darkness will keep you reading late into the night. Just remember to lock your doors." — Peter Russell, Hollywood story doctor, screenplay writer, and mentor

"A compelling journey by a master storyteller into the darkness of a mind possessed." — Dr. James Zender, Clinical and Forensic Psychologist, Author

"Bryant has scribbled a 'black belt' thriller, showcasing her immense talent, ambition with technique, and wonderfully wild imagination. But more importantly, it's readable as hell." — Joshua Mohr, One of O Magazine's Top 10 reads of 2009 and a *San Francisco Chronicle* best-seller

"Transport yourself into the mind and life of a serial killer in this unique and harrowing novel. Bryant's fascinating spin may start a whole new genre of the psychological thriller." — Peter Vronsky. Author of *Sons of Cain: A History of Serial Killers*

Pre-Publication Awards . . .

- Page-Turner Awards: eBook Finalist
- Reader's Favorites 5-star book award
- San Francisco Book Festival Award: Honorable Mention
- New York Book Festival Award: First Place scifi/horror
- Paris Book Festival Award: Honorable Mention

THE DARKNESS

Gary –
Writing is easier
Than watching. Thats
For sure!

Robbi

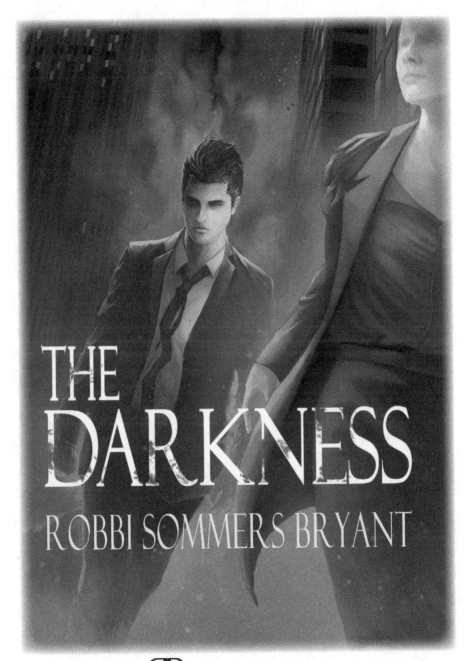

THE
DARKNESS

ROBBI SOMMERS BRYANT

Dusty Rose Books
Bedazzled Ink Publishing Company • Fairfield, California

© 2021 Robbi Sommers Bryant

All rights reserved. No part of this publication may be reproduced or transmitted in any means, electronic or mechanical, without permission in writing from the publisher.

978-1-949290-50-9 paperback

Cover Design
by
Ricardo Herrera

Dusty Rose Books
a division of
Bedazzled Ink Publishing Company
Fairfield, California
http://www.bedazzledink.com

ACKNOWLEDGMENTS

Thank you to the following for their support and skills during this project:
Lloyd Bryant for remarkable story-development support.
Belinda Riehl for her eagle-eye editing skills.
Arlene Battishill for intelligent developmental support.
Barbara Cottrell for her time and good advice as a beta reader
Ricardo Herrera excellent cover design.
Peter Russell extraordinary writing mentor.
One Stop for Writers for character development
Redwood Writers for always being there.
Bedazzled Ink for awesome publishing.

"When this monster entered my brain, I will never know . . .
Maybe you can stop him. I can't.
He has already chosen his next victim."
—Dennis Rader, BTK Killer

"I was born with the devil in me. I could not help the fact that I was a murderer,
no more than the poet can help the inspiration to sing—I was born with the
'Evil One' standing as my sponsor beside the bed where I was ushered into the
world, and he has been with me since."
—H. H. Holmes, The Beast of Chicago

About a week before Ted Bundy abducted and killed two girls on the same day in Washington State, his girlfriend thought he seemed odd. He inexplicably pushed her out of a raft into icy water and made no move to help her get out. "His face had gone blank," she later wrote, "as though he was not there at all. I had a sense that he wasn't seeing me."

To several of his post-arrest interviewers years later (William Hagmaier, Robert Keppel, Steven Michaud), Bundy described a malignant being—an "entity"—that emerged from him whenever he was tense or drunk.

Defense investigator Joe Aloi seemed to have gotten a clear view. While they were talking, he suddenly noticed an odor emanate from Bundy as his face and body contorted. "I felt that negative electricity," Aloi said, "and along with that came that smell." Aloi was suddenly terrified that Bundy would kill him.

Bundy said that during these encounters some malignant part of his personality took over—he called it "the entity"—and it was looking for satisfaction.

—Katherine Ramsland Ph.D. *Psychology Today Blog*: https://www.psychologytoday.com/us/blog/shadow-boxing/201309/bundys-demon-part-i, "Bundy's Demon: Part I," Sept 01, 2013

CHAPTER 1

THUNDER SLAMMED, AND lightning broke the sky. Edward Olson glanced at the flash that lit up the closed wood blinds. Without a word, he sighed. He wasn't in the mood to dump a body by the river. Not in the pouring rain. But the urge to strangle Cynthia Langford wouldn't let go. Edward tried to resist. He really did. He glanced at Cynthia, who sat next to him on his couch like a doe-eyed deer.

Couldn't he have an occasional date without the pressure to kill?

But The Darkness, an entity only Edward could see, had its own agenda. The creature perched on top of the coat rack—head hung low, shoulders hunched. As if it were all a game, the beast *click-clacked* its upper and lower beak. *Click-clack. Click-clack.* With a lift, it flapped its spiked wings, whooshed across the room, and landed on Edward's shoulder.

Edward glanced at his shadowy nemesis, a foot-tall creature with a beak, talons, and bat-shaped wings that could spread double its size when the damn thing flew—looking more like a thorn-covered Pterodactyl than a large bird. Its teeth, sharp as broken glass and vampiric, created a sense of desperate evil. *A good candidate for Satan's favorite pet*, Edward often thought.

Click-clack. Click-clack. Click-clack.

The nonstop sound grated Edward's nerves causing a hard tension to coil through him. He felt wound up and ready to pounce. And The Darkness wouldn't shut up. Always push-push-pushing Edward into a rage. If only the creature would disappear. He often daydreamed of living in a world unhampered by the monstrosity and its cravings. He tried to imagine himself with problems like a bad job, a broken-down car, or a steep mortgage. But his fraternity in life had members like Theodore "Ted" Bundy, Son-of-Sam David Berkowitz, and Blind-Torture-Kill murderer, Dennis Rader—all plagued by entities that forced them to kill.

Click-clack. Click-clack.

Edward's jaw clenched, and he swiped at the creature on his shoulder. The Darkness squawked, zoomed around the room, and landed on the other shoulder—its talons sunk deep.

As if it had a mind of its own, Edward's heel pumped up and down. His head pounded. *Leave me alone*, Edward thought—the words whizzed in his mind like a violent hurricane. The intensity of his need gnawed at him until he had no choice.

Edward glanced at Cynthia and muttered, "Can you excuse me a sec?"

"Sure, doll." Cynthia kissed his cheek. "Hurry back," she cooed. "I miss you already." She batted her hooded eyes.

Kill her, The Darkness insisted and leaped onto the coat rack.

Edward peered at the malicious creature as it snapped its beak open and shut, open and shut—escalating—becoming harsher, louder. Each *click* and *clack* taunted him. He felt as if a torture device was stretching his skin.

At one time, Edward thought he would get used to the click-clacking, but that never happened. The repetitive sound fucked with him like a hungry mosquito serenading an ear until it drove him into a rage. Edward curled his hands into fists, dug his nails into his palms, and sprang from the couch. As he barged toward the kitchen, he focused on maintaining control.

Just get me to the kitchen before I snap. But the ruthless shadow was already in the kitchen. Waiting. *Click-clacking*. The beast snorted then ground its jagged teeth together. The crunch of bone on bone—hideous.

Trying to get ahead of the terrible compulsion, Edward grabbed a bottle of Johnnie Walker Blue and gulped a shot. Sometimes it cooled him down.

But not tonight.

A zap of recklessness jolted through him.

Edward paced. Another shot.

And the *click-clacking*. The racket infuriated him. He needed a break.

"What should we watch?" Cynthia called from the screening room.

Edward had planned a quiet night—pizza and a movie—until The Darkness opened its cruel beak. And now, not even allowing Edward a chance to choose a film, the entity put him to the test.

Click-clack, click-clack.

Would you fucking stop? Edward slammed the scotch bottle against the Italian tile counter so hard it shattered. Glass and whiskey flew across the floor.

"Are you okay?" Cynthia's voice swirled from the other room.

And The Darkness—again with the beak clicking. The sounds ricocheted from wall to wall. Edward knew only one thing would ease the wrath that boiled inside him. Only one antidote could heal the sickness that cursed him.

"Edward?" Cynthia called.

Her voice wove between the booming sounds in Edward's head. His blue eyes, now black as death, focused as he strutted into the entertainment room. He no longer saw Cynthia. He no longer cared. She was nothing.

"Edward, what's wrong?"

Her shrill voice seemed too much to bear. And the incessant clicking, then crunching of the teeth drove him mad. He grabbed Cynthia by the neck and squeezed.

Cynthia's eyes filled with confused terror.

The Darkness landed on Edward—dug its talons into Edward's back—and rode him hard. The snapping and *click-clacking* reached a crescendo.

Cynthia, kicking and gasping, struggled to escape, but Edward held her firm—his strength too much for her. Although the light faded from her eyes, Cynthia refused to stop fighting.

Edward liked it when they struggled. It added to the drama.

The choking went on until Cynthia lost consciousness. Edward let go and slapped her until she came to. At first, she seemed disoriented, but seconds later, she tried to scream. His large hands went right to her throat—squeezing until she passed out again. He brought her back. Then strangled her once more. He took pleasure in blacking them out then reviving them.

It's like playing chess with Death.

Edward's smile turned vicious, and he skidded into a frenzy. He tightened his hands around Cynthia's neck. Trying to untangle herself from his grip, she kicked. But Edward hung on. Squeezing the life out of . . . of . . . whoever the hell she was . . . until she succumbed. Burst blood vessels in the whites of her eyes looked like veils of red lace. Her tongue turned a tell-all blue. Small marks dotted her neck.

Edward fell back onto the couch, the kill rushing through him. He howled like the predator he was. He was so drunk with pleasure he felt as if he could float with the clouds, dance with autumn leaves, sleep on the sea. The sensation lasted a minute, sometimes less. Didn't matter. Those seconds of ecstasy, those seconds of freedom, were worth the hassle of getting the body to the river in the rain. Mud or not.

The Darkness lifted from Edward's back, stretched its wings, and disappeared into a gloomy corner of the room. Heady from the release, Edward pulled himself back into the now. Back to Cynthia, sprawled on the couch like a discarded rag doll.

Edward glanced at the clock. No wonder he was hungry. He picked up the takeout menu—pepperoni or sausage? He couldn't decide. Hell, he had no idea what Cynthia preferred. To be fair, he ordered a half-and-half with a side of garlic fries then turned on the TV. Scrolling through the movies, he settled on *Sleepless in Seattle*. Romantic comedy, his favorite.

STARTLED, EDWARD JERKED out of a dream. It took a few moments to orient himself. He was still in the screening room—one arm wrapped around Cynthia Langford's body. The red light from the clock cast a hollow glow. On TV, a shady-eyed preacher tried his best to sell God.

2:45 a.m.

Edward peeked between the blinds and appraised the early morning. Moon slivered. Slight drizzling. He could make it down to the river and back dry if he wore rain gear—another hassle. He lifted Cynthia and hauled her out to his three-car garage. Her stiffening body felt like a bag of cement, but he crammed her into the trunk and slammed it.

As he drove toward Cynthia's new resting place, Edward listened to de Senneville's music. Once parked, he fast-forwarded to "Mariage d'Amour," the perfect piece for carrying Cynthia's body down to the river's edge—she would have loved the romance of it all.

Edward took a moment to take in his surroundings. Low-lit industrial buildings stood like gravestones against the sky. The air was still, and the sound of the water gurgled like a death rattle. He lay Cynthia on the concrete and dirt silt and noticed her foot dangling in the water. *Would she mind?* A gentleman, he dragged the body toward the incline that led to the fence. Should he head home and return later? Or grab the tarp and have sex with her now?

BY THE TIME Edward dumped Cynthia and returned home, it was 4:30 a.m. His first class, Legal Writing, was less than a few hours away. *Shit. The last thing I want is to ruin my buzz.* He decided, instead, to take a road trip to Las Vegas. It would be a luxury to escape the bloated, dull Seattle clouds and the stresses of being a student.

Edward turned onto I-84, heading east. He debated how long he wanted to be on the road. Most times, he drove to Vegas. He'd lose himself in reflective thought, dissecting his behavior and mood. Sometimes he'd focus on finding the next woman. Today, he felt like driving for its own sake. Take in the scenery. Enjoy the desert heat.

Law school was a goddamn albatross. First, it was time-consuming, and second, at thirty, he was the oldest in the class. It would be hip to say he was an attorney, but he hadn't realized the work involved in becoming one. Shit. Why not drop out of school and just *say* he was a lawyer? How hard would it be to add law books and fake files to his office? It's not like he needed the money.

His long-lost grandmother had skipped his bitch-of-a-dead-mother and had left her fortune to him. The six million-plus allowed Edward to live well. He had an estate on five acres, and women adored the seclusion—that is until they screamed for help, and nobody came. The pool, the screening room, the home gym, and the woods that surrounded the 4500-square-foot house were only a few features his luxury home offered.

Edward decided he'd stay at the Bellagio. Sometimes he'd meet a woman at the pool, take her to Sinatra's for Veal Parmigiana, maybe catch a show, and walk her back to the hotel. But this trip, he'd spend time at the casinos, shop at Caesar's, and cruise the streets. There are always women in Vegas looking for some fun.

After two days, the death of a hooker, and three thousand in winnings, Edward headed back to Seattle. Instead of working out in his home gym, he stopped at his health club near the University.

CHAPTER 2

AFTER A BUSY Monday at work, twenty-six-year-old Cate Derry headed to the gym. She'd been a nurse at the University of Washington's Harborview Medical Center for a month and was now familiar with the protocols. Although worn out, she convinced herself to get on the elliptical trainer for thirty minutes. She put in her earbuds, turned on her music, and claimed the last open machine. Next to her, a Dylan McDermott look-alike glanced at her, smiled like he knew her, and returned to his workout. In trendy workout clothes, he looked like new money. His tousled dark hair—shaved close on the sides and longer on top—highlighted his haunting blue eyes. His cheekbones were high fashion. Oh, yes, she'd seen his type before and was certain women threw themselves at him.

But not Cate.

She pulled herself back to her workout and kept her pace while Lady Gaga sang. Perspiration cleansed the stress she carried in her neck and shoulders. Critical care was for strong-willed and tough-minded nurses. Cate, however, vowed she would leave her career if she ever felt hardened.

Cate's workout slowed from the fifteen-minute cooldown to a complete stop. The guy next to her wound down as well.

"Looks like you worked your butt off," he said, his voice casual.

Cate pulled the earbuds out. "I'm sorry, I . . . ah . . . what did you say?" She blushed. Her lack of experience with men presented as social awkwardness. She didn't like small talk. Didn't have the gift.

"You're new here?" The Dylan-McDermott-of-the-gym asked.

"Nope. I usually come around six. I didn't realize the gym would be empty later in the evening."

"Don't get used to it. It's an off-night."

"Right." Cate stepped off the elliptical and blotted her face with a towel.

"What do you do that keeps your workout late?" He grabbed his towel.

"I'm a nurse." Her anxiety revved to high, and she glanced toward the locker room. *Okay, Gotta run,* she thought she'd say. But he'd steered the conversation forward before she could speak.

"Impressive. Hey, I like the ponytail."

She'd pulled her straight hair back that morning—part of her daily routine–and put her ponytail near the crown of her head. Made her look spunky, which she liked. The scrubs in her locker were a cheery blue with a small-rabbits-and-carrots design. The blue pants matched. Cate felt cartoon tops made her less intimidating to patients and highlighted the difference between her and the bully nurses who ran the fifth-floor Critical Care Unit.

Well, say something. Don't just stand there like an idiot. "Keeps it out of my face." Cate glanced at the two yellow balls in his elliptical's cupholder. "What do you do with your balls?" *Holy cheeses. Did I just say that?* Cate felt her face heat.

He laughed. "Well, that's an interesting question."

"I know. I meant . . . I didn't think before—"

"Works out my hands," he said with a wink. "I like to keep them strong." He picked up a ball and squeezed it. "I'm a defense attorney. You never know when you might need to punch an obnoxious prosecutor."

"Smart *and* funny." *Fine. Enough small talk.* It was the perfect time to untangle herself from this conversation. "Gotta run." She headed toward the women's locker room.

"Hey, wait." He hurried to her side. "Is your name Caitlyn Derry?"

"Do I know you?"

"We . . . uh . . . had a class together. I dropped it after three days, but I remember you."

"Really?" Cate eyed him. "What class?"

"What class?" he repeated. "Biology. I thought about medical school."

"Good memory." *How could he possibly remember me?* Cate thought. But it didn't matter—not really. "Well, nice to see you again," she mumbled, still walking.

"How about dinner Saturday night?"

"Sorry." She felt her face flush as she shook her head.

He caught up with her. "Lunch?"

"I don't date."

"Coffee and a bagel?"

Deep within, she felt an undercurrent of magnetism she didn't understand; even so, she stopped, turned toward him, and smiled. "I'm sorry. No."

CATE STEPPED OUT of the gym to the parking lot and moaned. Her back tire sat flat against the ground. "Oh, sheets!" She tossed her gym bag across the asphalt. "Now what?" A tear welled in her eye. It was times like this that she missed her dad more than usual.

"Looks like you've got a bit of a problem. Let me give you a hand."

Cate turned to find Dylan-of-the-gym right behind her. He'd crept upon her without making a sound. *Oh God, did he see me having my tantrum?* She tried to be nonchalant as she walked across the lot to retrieve her bag.

He squatted next to the tire. "There's a nail in the sidewall. You got a spare?"

"Yes, but I have no idea how to change a tire."

"Don't you worry. The cavalry has arrived."

Cate watched the chivalrous stranger take off the flat and screw on the spare. She had to admit; he *was* gorgeous with his contagious smile, sculpted nose, and commanding eyes. The right height for her five-foot-five frame—he looked just under six feet with arms as strong as her dad's. And the guy seemed just as sweet.

After he finished changing the flat, he stood and stretched. "How about that coffee and bagel?"

And what could Cate say after he'd rescued her from what would have been an exasperating night? "Just coffee and a bagel?"

The man nodded and crossed his heart. "I promise."

"Sure, okay."

"You know where Bean and Bagel is?" He wiped his hands together.

"Fortieth and fifteenth, right?"

"Does tomorrow morning work for you? Say, seven?"

"See you then," Cate replied. "Hey, thanks again." Already, she wished she'd said no. She imagined them at a table for two at Bean and Bagel. What would they talk about? The pressure would be excruciating. The small talk unbearable. What would he think if she had nothing fascinating to say?

CATE ENTERED BEAN and Bagel, her strawberry-blonde hair in the ponytail he'd liked. Tiny, pink-elephant barrettes captured most of the stray hairs. Her ivory skin showed-off her Pacific-blue eyes, her nose was lightly sprinkled with freckles.

He was already at a table. A bouquet of daffodils lay on top.

"For you." He stood and handed her the lemon-yellow flowers.

"Oh my, they're stunning."

Although this gesture suggested more than "just coffee," Cate no longer cared. Once again, she felt that same familiarity as she had at the gym. It was as if they were cohorts sharing a secret no one else knew. *Why?*

"I might as well tell you my name, Caitlyn." He laughed. "I'm Edward." He offered his well-manicured hand.

"I go by Cate." She liked his firm handshake. "Last night, I realized that I hadn't gotten your name. Goofy, huh?" *Goofy, huh. What a ridiculous thing to say,* she silently admonished herself.

"*I* like Cait*lyn*." He smiled. "So, you're a nurse." He seemed to appraise her scrubs as he pulled out a chair for her. Cartoon elephants decorated her top. The pink pants matched the color of the elephants.

"I work in critical care." Her voice cracked.

"Next time I need critical care, I'll be sure to ask for you." Edward winked.

"Not so fast. Gosh, I'd feel awful if I accidentally killed you." She giggled. "Do you like being an attorney?"

"All smoke and mirrors," Edward said.

"What's your specialty?"

"My specialty?" His voice was as silky as expensive stockings. "Federal criminal defense—forfeiture."

It surprised Caitlyn how easy it was to chat with Edward. He exuded confidence while remaining humble. A take-charge man yet respectful. Every subject he mentioned, she had a response. He made her comfortable. Enjoying herself, Cate almost relaxed.

"I'm thinking sesame bagel, toasted. And cream cheese. What about you, Caitlyn?"

"I go by *Cate*," she repeated, her voice firm. Ever since they took her father away, she went by Cate. Period. "I'll have the same with coffee." As Cate placed her menu back in the slot, the back of her hand knocked over her glass. Water soaked her pants.

"Sunny beaches. That's cold."

"Sunny beaches?" Edward laughed, blotting the table with paper napkins.

"I don't swear," she replied. She pulled a wad of napkins from the holder. "My dad never swore. I liked that about him."

"So sunny beaches is Cait*lyn* talk for son of a bitch?" He emphasized the "lyn" in her name.

"It's *Cate*," she mumbled, looking down at her wet lap.

"What got you into nursing?" Edward sopped up the water on the table with a handful of napkins and waved to the waiter.

"I've always wanted to help people. It's my life's purpose." She peeked at the clock. "Heck. Where did the time go? I've got to get to work."

"Jesus, it takes forever to get a waiter," Edward complained.

Cate shrugged and stood. "Sorry, I can't stay."

"How about a picnic Saturday instead?" Edward asked. "You know, a raincheck?"

"I—"

"It's only fair." Edward handed her a napkin and pen.

Cate hesitated. Would she regret giving him her number? She glanced at his foot tap, tap, tapping against the linoleum floor. Obviously, he was as nervous as she was.

She scribbled her number and her name, *Cate,* which she underlined several times to reinforce that she went by Cate not Caitlyn.

Edward picked up the napkin, said the number out loud, and repeated her name. "Caitlyn."

"*Cate,*" she said, irritated that he refused to use her name correctly. *Was he stubborn? Not listening?* It was enough for her to consider canceling.

But he looked her straight in the eyes and said, "Caitlyn—a beautiful name for a beautiful woman."

Cate reached for the bouquet and smiled.

CHAPTER 3

A FEW DAYS after he met Caitlyn for coffee, Edward felt battered by the entity and its ever-increasing cravings. If he didn't hunt when The Darkness demanded, he'd be stricken with a tortuous withdrawal that was a challenge to hide. His body would feel jittery. His teeth would clamp together, and the muscles around his jaws would thicken. He'd feel on edge and ready to fight. Since he'd killed a hooker in Vegas, the last six weeks had been tolerable—he'd only needed an occasional shot of Johnnie Blue to take the edge off.

Anxiety pummeled him. If he wasn't tapping his foot, he was jiggling his knee up and down. His stomach felt turned inside out, and he struggled not to gnaw at his nails. Revved up, but having no way to release the building tension, caused the need to pace. His mind spun. If he forced his jaw to relax, his teeth chattered. As if itching and not finding the right place to scratch, there was no relief in sight.

In the law library, Edward leaned back on the chair's back legs and chewed on his pen. If he wanted to pass tomorrow's exam, he'd better study. He had a massive amount to learn. But he couldn't concentrate. The creature had become greedy and ready for more.

Edward glanced around the room. Everyone seemed engrossed in their work. The small lamps in their computer cubbies glowed. Students at the tables sat in groups of four. Edward wondered how it would feel to be like them, free of the entity that riddled his psyche. Why was he saddled with The Darkness' soulless needs? Why couldn't he just fit in?

I'm sick of studying, Edward thought, bringing the front legs of his chair to the floor.

Across the room, a woman gathered her books. He smiled at her. She glanced at him and turned away.

What's the matter with people today? Can't they take a moment to acknowledge each other? He peeked at his watch. Back to her. Back to his watch. She put on her windbreaker and headed for the exit. Before stepping outside, she reached into her backpack, brought out a red polka dot hat, and put it on.

The Darkness stretched into its wingspan and flapped its wings. *Click-clack.*

"Shut up," Edward growled under his breath.

Knowing he should finish the assignment, aware that another low grade would doom him, he collected his notes, put his books in his briefcase, and headed to the exit. A melancholy sky canopied Seattle, and a slight chill crisped the air.

"Hey," he called to the woman with the polka dot accessory, now at the corner.

She turned, struggling to hold on to her hat against the stubborn spring breeze.

"Crappy weather," charming Edward said as he sprinted toward her.

The woman watched her hat tumble into the street. "Shit."

The fiend riding Edward's back hung on as Edward zigzagged between cars to recover the hat. He handed her the rain hat with a bow. "Milady."

"Wow, and I thought chivalry was dead."

Edward broke into the Temptations song, "Treat Her Like a Lady," adding a couple double steps and a tight turn.

The woman laughed. "You should audition for *America's Got Talent.*"

"Was that you in the law library?" Edward's intuitive nature kept him even-keeled, which afforded him time to examine the emotions of others. He'd learned to exhibit the social graces expected of a star-quality lawyer.

"Yeah, first year."

"Me, too." Edward flashed a smile. "Can I give you a ride?"

"Sorry, I don't take candy from strangers." She smiled.

"I'm not a stranger; I'm a fellow law student."

"Nope," she replied. "I'm waiting for a ride, but thanks."

Her quick refusal added fuel to his already heightened need for release, but Edward stayed composed.

"How about coffee then?"

"I'm married." She shrugged.

Fucking bitch. The Darkness, as black as hell's walls, swiped Edward's back. *I want her.*

Who is she to discount me? Edward replied. *She can't have a cup coffee with a fellow law student because there's a husband? Where do people come up with these ridiculous rules?*

He thought back to foster-home living. When he was three years old, his drugged-out, prostitute mother traded him for a bag of heroin. Passed around like a beat-up toy, sexually and physically assaulted for two years, Edward had burn marks on his belly, a broken rib, and bruises on his back when someone finally had enough sense to call Child Protective Services. He stayed with a foster family whose list of rules, written in thick block letters, was posted on a bulletin board in the stark and loveless home. Before dinner, he would be called to face Mother Sue for the daily evaluation. If he'd broken any rules, she'd yank down his pants and gave him a hard smack with a belt.

Edward could take the pain, but the pulling down of the pants in front of three giggling girls filled him with rage too intense to contain. At first, the fury manifested as temper tantrums and bedwetting, but as he got older, it escalated to fighting and refusing to follow the rules. And just for fun, he set fires.

For a moment, a storm of red blinded Edward. Too cranked up to let some mousy law student—who thought she was better than him—get away, he considered following her, giving her what she deserved. But a Mercedes pulled up, and the girl climbed in. Frustrated, Edward walked to his car, got in, and cruised the surrounding area for prey.

Sometimes the opportunity refused to show.

The Darkness jumped to the passenger seat from the back and preened itself. After separating a few feathers, it clucked and looked up. *I want a fix.*

Too bad. Edward didn't hide his irritation.

The beast leaned over and pecked deep into Edward's arm.

What the fuck? Edward gave The Darkness a light slap on the beak. He knew not to go any further. *Stop it.*

I've been patient. Enough is enough. The Darkness pinched the flesh of Edward's arm then jumped out of reach.

I swear to God, I'm going to—

God? The shadow smirked. *You think you and God belong in the same sentence?* The spiked creature jumped from Edward's shoulder to the seat. *Click-clack.*

Give me a break, will you? Edward muttered. *We'll have better luck when the sun sets.*

The Darkness pushed a wayward spike on his wing in place with his beak. *Click-clack. Click-clack. Click-clack.*

Stop! The continual clatter strained Edward's nerves. It was hard enough for him to wait for the kill without the goddamn Darkness pestering him.

But the black entity wouldn't let up. It hopped onto Edward's shoulder and whispered in his ear. *Let's do it now.*

Edward clamped his hands onto the steering wheel so tight that his knuckles ached. Images of his recent assaults twisted in his mind. The Darkness relished the killing, but for Edward, it was the terror in the eyes; the fading irises; the scream unable to push its way out the girl's blue lips—all of it. Every goddamned second of it. He pulled over to the curb and screamed as loud as he could. Anything to calm his need. He felt like a junkie needing his fix. A glance at the clock—less than an hour until sundown.

Up ahead, he saw her. A girl walked alone, her back to Edward. He and The Darkness exchanged a glance then broke into sinister laughs.

"Lookie here," Edward said, motioning to the girl. "And you say God doesn't care."

Another round of snickering.

The sun dipped into the horizon, the orange and yellows suffocating as they drained from the sky. Edward cruised by, appraised the girl, then slowed. A little younger than he liked them—she was maybe sixteen—but a fix was a fix. He lowered the passenger window. "Excuse me." He pulled the car to the curb.

The girl walked to the passenger side. "Hey." Her glittery pink lipstick sparkled, contrasting with her black eyeliner drawn thick.

A fine mist of rain blurred the windshield. Edward clicked the wipers once to clear his view of the road. As empty as a demon's heart, the pavement seemed to stretch into the horizon. Oncoming clouds swallowed the sky, and the night crept toward the horizon.

"Do you know how to get to the highway from here? I've gotten myself turned around."

"Don't you have GPS?" the girl said. She flipped her long dark hair out of her eyes.

Edward shrugged. "Left my cell at home. Duh."

"It's not too far," she said, glancing up the road.

As if on cue, large drops of rain splattered against the windshield.

"Shit." The girl pulled up her hoodie.

"Hop in," Edward said with his killer smile. "I'll give you a ride." He pushed the button, and the doors unlocked.

The girl settled in the seat and flashed Edward a smile. "I've got a joint."

"Would you rather vape?" He popped open the glove compartment and pulled out a vape pen. "This is great stuff."

"Sure thing," the girl said with a giggle. She had no idea she was flirting with evil—no idea she was a few hundred breaths from death.

The rain danced on the roof like a clumsy tap dancer. "I'm older than I look," she purred.

"Is that right?"

"I'm gonna be seventeen in three months."

"Wow, you don't look a day over—"

"I hear it all the time."

"Here." Edward handed her the vape pen, put the car in drive, and drove into the rain.

The girl took a hit, handed it to Edward, and looked at him with her Cleopatra eyes. After a deep inhalation, he passed the vape back to her. As she breathed in, he scanned the back seat—damn, he hated not being prepared. *Ah, there.* He reached into his back seat, grabbed the hammer, and looked at the girl.

"Have you ever seen a $250 hammer? I got it this morning. It's titanium. Cool, huh?"

He handed her the hammer and took the vape. "Hey, what's your name?"

"Marlise. Wow, this is good shit. I'm already stoned big time."

Edward passed the pen and took the hammer back.

"Why is that hammer so expensive?"

Edward's heartbeat cranked. The girl's life force smelled sweet.

"Titanium is expensive, but it's lighter than steel. And a swing transfers 97 percent of the energy as opposed to a steel hammer's 70 percent. At least that's what the sales guy said."

"What are you going to use it for?"

"I'm going to knock you out with it, so I can kill you when you wake up," Edward said, his voice flat.

"Ha, ha," Marlise said, her smile gone.

Edward's jungle eyes sized up his prey.

"Hey, come on, this isn't funny." Fear swirled in her eyes.

"I think it is." Edward swerved off the road, jammed on the brakes, pulled her head down, and swung the hammer. *Shit, that sales guy was right—97 percent and lightweight.* He chuckled along with his dark companion. Edward drove out of Seattle to finish the deed.

CHAPTER 4

TEN O'CLOCK, SATURDAY morning. Cate sipped her second cup of coffee when the doorbell rang. As she headed for the front door, Pipsqueak ran around her feet like a dust mop.

"Quit yapping, Pipsqueak," Cate said as she tried to step around the small mutt she'd rescued three years ago.

Through the peephole, she saw her eighty-year-old neighbor, Ruby Valin, with a head full of curlers, a bright blue and gold scarf wrapped around them, large gold hoop earrings that hung low, and thick red lipstick breaching the borders of her lips. Her penciled-in dark brows contrasted with her brassy-red hair. Cate reflected on the day Ruby had shown her how to "doll herself up." The result? Cate had looked like a hooker with a thing for clowns.

"Morning." Cate opened the door for Ruby. "Want coffee?"

"Well, since you asked." Ruby was already in the entranceway. "Hey, little Pip." She bent down to pet Pipsqueak, who jumped with joy.

"Okay, Pipsy." Ruby lifted the pup into her arms, and he covered her in kisses. "I fed Pipsqueak last night." She swished into the living room where Cate's clothes laid on the floor near the scarlet 1940s-style couch. "Another late one, huh?"

"That's the life of a critical-care nurse." Cate gathered her jacket, shoes, and clothes and piled them on a gold vintage chair.

The quaint living room featured a brick fireplace, two easy chairs, and a couch. A carved coffee table sat in front of the sofa with three red and gold flowers inlaid in the wood. On the walls hung several framed prints by the artist Edward Hopper, her favorite, *At the Movies*, hung above the mantle. Closed gold drapes covered a large picture window that looked out to the flowering front yard. And in the corner, a fifty-inch TV.

Once in the kitchen, Cate poured a cup of coffee, added two teaspoons of sugar, and a dash of cream for Ruby.

"Can you take Pip for a walk around dinner tonight?" Cate sat across the kitchen table from Ruby.

"Girlfriend, you need to get yourself a life outside the hospital." Ruby sat Pipsqueak on the floor.

"Actually . . ." Cate felt her face burn. She wasn't one to share much personal information, but Ruby was different. A close friend of Cate's now-deceased mother, Ruby had been a strong support for Cate.

"Well, I'll be. You're blushing."

"I have a date," Cate mumbled as they walked into the living room and sat down. "We're walking—"

"Wait, wait, wait. *You* have a date?" Ruby grabbed Cate's arm. "Since when are you dating?"

"We're going to Green Lake. I don't know why I agreed to go. I've already said everything on the phone. What happens if my mind goes blank? Why did I do this to myself? I'm happy as things are. It's better to be—"

"Slow down, *bubeleh*," Ruby interjected. "First things first. Who?"

"I met him at the gym on Thursday night." Cate shifted in her chair. "His name is Edward."

"And *you* said yes to a date?"

"He wouldn't let up until I agreed to bagels." Cate stirred her coffee. "We met at Bean and Bagel yesterday morning and talked on the phone last night."

Ruby leaned in. "And?"

"I don't know what it is about him . . ." Cate drifted off for a moment.

"Who would have thought?"

"I traded shifts with Anabelle."

"That isn't the norm for diehard Nurse Cate." Ruby laughed.

"I needed a break anyway. Those unexpected deaths in Critical Care over the last few months have the fifth floor spooked. Everyone is tight-lipped, but I overheard Supervisor Bloom discuss the 'confidential' problem with Director Stein. Bloom is on everyone's tush. Triple micro-managing."

"Well, you've always said she was a 'be-ach'—and not so sunny, that one." Ruby picked up Pipsqueak. "Looks dreary today. Supposed to rain."

"Oh, no. What happens if it rains? We can't sit outside in a storm," Cate moaned. She didn't like last-minute changes; they unnerved her. And she was already a wreck—*what would they talk about? What if she had nothing left to say?*

"Calm down. Worrying about what may happen is a waste of time. You lose today when your mind sits in tomorrow. Best conversation? You ask the questions, and he answers. Get him to talk about himself. What he likes to do for fun. Where he hangs out. That sort of *bubba maisa*."

"You and your Yiddish." Cate smiled then tapped a fingernail on the coffee table. "Why did I say yes? Talking on the phone is more comfortable. I should have left it that. I'm not ready for this. The last thing I need is a man."

"*Bubbe*, why do you have that in your head? Love can open your world in a whole new way. Ever since we found out about your father, you've closed down."

"But they took him away like a can of trash," Cate muttered.

"It's not like he didn't deserve it," Ruby replied. "You know that."

"Even so, he was my dad, and I loved him, no matter what." Cate clicked on the TV and turned up *Dr. Phil*. "Saturday reruns on the Oprah Channel."

"Gotta love that Dr. Phil," Ruby added.

"I like this episode, 'Lies and Betrayal.'"

"I married a con artist," the woman on TV told Dr. Phil. "He said he was a doctor, had millions of dollars, and was dying of cancer."

"She married me for my money," the rodent of a man replied.

"Let's watch," Cate said, grateful the subject of her father was off the table. Ruby glanced at the TV. "The guy's a sociopath."

Not knowing if Ruby referred to her father or the louse on TV, Cate mumbled, "Perhaps so."

CHAPTER 5

"WOW. YOU'RE A real knockout." Edward gave Cate the once-over while a yipping Pipsqueak ran in circles around his feet. Edward stepped past Pip and gave Cate a light hug.

Cate couldn't help noticing his designer jeans, sharp sports shirt, and expensive sneakers. He was *GQ* all the way. "Pipsqueak, sit."

The dog continued to bark but stopped the loop around Edward's feet.

"Thanks for the compliment." *Well? Say something clever.* "Yum, you smell good. What cologne are you wearing?" *Oh, my gosh, I sound like an idiot.*

"Ah, my little-known secret. Tonka 25."

"I like it." *I should say I have a headache. I should put my hand to my head and stumble to a chair.* "Would you like to come in for some homemade lemonade?" *Gosh darn, why the heck did I say that? There's still time for a sudden migraine.*

Edward scanned the living room. "Nice place." His eyes stopped at the framed replica of Hopper's *New York Movie.* "What a coincidence. I love Hopper's work."

"Really? What's your favorite," Cate motioned for Edward to sit on the sofa.

"*Room in New York,*" Edward replied as he sat on the plush cushion.

"So, is that a yes for the lemonade?"

As Cate headed for the kitchen, she glanced at her reflection in the full-length mirror framed in gilded gold. She wore a pair of black capri pants, a crinkled gingham boy-shirt in pink and white, and a black cardigan. *He thinks I'm a knockout.*

CAITLYN RETURNED FROM the kitchen with a pitcher of lemonade.

"I bought a henway today," Edward said as she set glasses on the table.

"What's a henway?"

"About six pounds."

Caitlyn burst into laughter. "That's a good one."

Edward suspected she'd like a guy who kidded around. It was a gift—the art of figuring out what a person needed and reeling them in within minutes. An expert in seduction, he flattered women by making it seem like he understood them like no one else ever had. Women thought "soulmate" when Edward turned on the charm.

But with Caitlyn, Edward's reasons had nothing to do with a kill. She was the prize he'd been searching for since his mid-twenties. She was the right woman, the only woman, for him. Edward couldn't believe his good fortune. After all this time, his life had circled back to *her*. Caitlyn Derry.

Since his early teens, Edward had followed the string of murders and felt a kinship with Patrick Derry, the infamous Lace Ribbon Killer. An international attorney who traveled extensively, Derry had a high-profile law practice yet in the shadows, had been one of Seattle's most prolific serial killers.

Edward had watched the news stories. A strangled woman found by the river, another in the hills, a lace ribbon tied around each woman's neck. *The Seattle Times* had daily updates, and he heard his foster mother gossip about Seattle women afraid to go out because of this guy. Not only did Edward clip every newspaper article and keep a diary of Derry's kills, he also spent his free time daydreaming about tying women up and watching them die. After eight years of bodies being discovered around the Pacific Northwest, the FBI captured Derry.

It was an incredible shock when the community learned that intelligent and personable Patrick James Derry was responsible for the lasso of terror that had roped-in the residents. But not a shock for Edward, who was thrilled to find Derry was a regular guy.

Once convicted and sentenced to death, Patrick Derry received a plethora of letters from Edward, who vowed to watch out for Caitlyn, and after a while, Derry felt good about the kid and his loyalty. It had been twelve years since Derry's execution. Edward had lost track of Caitlyn when she'd graduated from nursing school and moved away. *Life has its reasons*, Edward had thought then and thought it now.

Edward had fantasized about meeting up with Caitlyn for years. He would become the man of her dreams. She liked Mozart, so Edward said he did too. She enjoyed carnivals, so did he. She was looking for a daddy figure—which is what he would be. Caitlyn Derry was the ultimate trophy.

After a few minutes, Edward delved deeper into Cate's psyche than he had on the phone. What were her dreams? (To be a doctor.) What did she fear? (Disappointing others.) Was she a happy child?

"What about you?" Caitlyn asked.

"My parents were killed in a car crash when I was three." *Lie.* "The nanny raised me." *Lie.* "But I had a happy childhood." *Lie. Lie. Lie.* "I came into a nice inheritance, though." Edward liked to throw in an occasional truth.

Twenty minutes of light chitchat had passed when Edward said, "Ready for our picnic?"

Caitlyn nodded, gave Pipsqueak a chew toy, and she and Edward headed out the door. Just as they reached Edward's silver Altima, a slamming sound from the house next door to Caitlyn's caused Edward to stop in his tracks. Smashed against the front window between bent blinds, an older woman with fiery-red hair offered a slight wave and raised her arms as if to say, "Whoops."

"Oh, dear." Caitlyn laughed. "She must have been peeking and slipped."

"Nosy neighbor?" Edward said, his fake laugh strained.

Caitlyn went red. "That's Ruby, my friend. Quirky."

"She knows about our date?" Edward opened the car door for Cate. This did not please him. "How close of a friend?" he said, as if nonchalant.

"She's my only real friend in Seattle; she helped my mom raise me after my dad . . . left. You must meet her. She's a real kick."

Edward came around to the driver's side. Ruby was someone to keep an eye on, friend or not.

THE SPRING DAY bloomed in Seattle. After a leisurely walk along the lake, Edward went back to the car and returned with a gold-trimmed navy blanket and a picnic basket filled with a loaf of French bread, caviar, cheeses, pate, a book of poems, and a bottle of sparkling apple cider.

"I'd ply you with expensive wine, but there's no alcohol allowed in the park."

"I'm not much of a drinker," Cate replied.

After a toast to happiness and a bite of bread and cheese, Caitlyn tiptoed toward a swallowtail butterfly resting on a wildflower. She almost reached it when she stumbled, and the butterfly—its yellow wings with black tiger stripes fluttering—lifted and soared away.

"Are you okay?" Edward hurried to help her up.

"I've fallen for a butterfly." Caitlyn laughed.

"No, *I've* fallen for a butterfly." Edward hugged Caitlyn.

Made for my arms.
Made for my kisses.
Made for my soul.

"That's lovely," Cate said. "Did you write that?"

Edward laughed. "That's Pablo Neruda."

The Darkness hung from a branch like an enormous bat. Eyes closed, it moved like a restless sleeper. Edward glanced at the beast and flashed on the agreement he'd made. He'd promised The Darkness he would satisfy all its urges if it would keep its goddamned beak to itself when Cate was around.

With a flap of his wings, The Darkness opened one eye and seemed to focus on Caitlyn as if she were a juicy rat. Edward kept a flask of his favorite scotch, Johnnie Blue, in his car. To take the edge off. To quiet his considerable agitation. He decided a couple gulps might be smart.

"I left my cell in the car," Edward lied. "Do you need anything?"

"No, I'm perfect."

"You'll be okay by yourself?"

"Of course, I will."

Edward gave Caitlyn a light kiss on the cheek and headed toward the parking lot.

CATE LEANED BACK on the blanket and let the warmth of the sun lull her into relaxation. Glad the rain had failed to appear, she enjoyed being cradled in the arms of the earth.

"Hey. Nice day, right?"

Cate sat up, shaded her eyes, and peered at the stranger hovering over her with a beer in his hand. She did a quick scan of her surroundings but didn't see Edward. Uncertain what to do, she shrugged.

"Mind if I join you."

"I'm with someone." Cate felt a tingling in her chest.

"I don't see anyone." His words slurred as if he'd finished a few beers already. "Finders keepers," he said with an exaggerated wink.

Cate didn't like being caught off-guard, especially by a drunk. "I'm not in the mood for company."

"Sure, you are." Almost losing his balance on the way down, he landed next to on her blanket. As if they were lovers, he put his arm around her shoulders. "Honey, you sure are a pretty bird."

Cate untangled from his arm, stood up, and backed away from the man who sloppily got to his feet and came toward her.

At that moment, Edward came into view.

"Edward," Cate shouted. "Need some help here."

"What the hell," Edward yelled and stormed toward the man like an enraged bull. He grabbed the interloper by the front of his t-shirt and slugged him with a brutal uppercut. The man fell, and Edward kicked him twice in the belly.

Just as Edward went to boot the guy in the head, Cate screamed, "Edward, no!"

"Nobody messes with you, Caitlyn. Not on my watch." Edward gave the guy one strong kick in the groin for good measure then bundled up the blanket while Cate put the food and drink into the basket.

A man, built like a refrigerator, approached them from behind. "Hey, buddy. Jesus Christ, you trying to kill that guy?"

"What's it to you?" Edward's eyes narrowed, and his hands clenched.

"If I were you, I'd step away," Cate said. "That jerk tried to hurt me. And this man"—She pointed to Edward—"is dangerous, so butt out."

Edward shot a surprised look at Cate, who smiled sweetly.

"Get the fuck out of here," Edward growled.

The burly man looked Edward in the eye. As if he could see the ungodly darkness that resided there, he said, "Whatever, dude," and walked away.

"Let's head over to Spud Fish and Chips. Been there?" Edward said as if nothing had happened.

But for Cate, something deep within her clicked, and a warm intoxication flowed through her. The last time anyone had ever protected her was her father. Nobody else could be trusted. Nobody else could ever penetrate the hard shell encasing Cate's psyche. For the first time since her father was taken away, she felt that perhaps someone could.

EDWARD'S MIND REELED. Caitlyn hadn't seemed appalled, frightened, or upset about his violent behavior. In fact, after the incident, he sensed a subtle change in her. She'd even grabbed his hand on the way back to the car. Was Caitlyn accepting of his behavior? Could it be possible to just be himself with her? This possibility brought him a sense of peace like he'd never experienced before.

Suddenly, the world seemed right.

At the restaurant, the creature clicked and clacked but only enough to put Edward on edge. Thinking ahead, Edward decided they should get takeout to be safe. After picking up their order, they rode to Caitlyn's place and ended up on her living room couch.

Edward sat with his arm around Caitlyn as she snuggled in close. *Like it should be. Like it always would be.* It was this moment Edward felt his wound-up nerves quiet.

But not for long.

Like lightning on a bleak snowy night, The Darkness broke the calm. A loud crackling and The Darkness opened its now blood-red eyes to take a covetous look at Caitlyn. Edward saw the creature prepare to lunge as it click-clacked repeatedly. The urge to put his hands around Caitlyn's slender neck overwhelmed him.

Horrified, Edward mumbled he'd be right back and hurried to his car. He grabbed the bottle of Johnnie Blue, opened it, took a swig, and headed back to the house with bottle in hand.

As Edward came through the front door, The Darkness flapped its outspread wings and swooped. Edward tensed as the demon clamped its talons around him. He attempted to shake the creature off, to no avail. Trying to connect with reason, Edward could only come up with a murky haze.

This was Caitlyn, serial killer Patrick Derry's daughter. She'd seen a hint of his violent nature and didn't seem to care. And now, as he sat next to Caitlyn, The Darkness wanted Edward to take her life?

Misery dripped from Edward as he blindly returned to the living room with his bottle of strength. *The goddamn fucking Darkness had no business eyeing her. This was a mistake. A horrendous mistake.*

"You okay?" Caitlyn asked.

The Darkness hooked deeper into Edward.

Click-clack.

The buildup, fast and harsh, sped out of control. *Stop*—the word echoed in Edward's mind.

Click-clack. Click-clack—the sound of Evil's flamenco shoes. As the clatter of noise neared its peak, Edward prepared to lunge.

The churning in his head screamed.

The *click-clack* blasted around the room, bouncing back louder.

His heart thumped. His shallow breaths cycled rapidly.

He reached for Caitlyn. So adorable. So sweet.

Do it. Do it, The Darkness demanded.

The malicious creature sliced through Edward like a death-soaked bullet. All Edward could think of was the release. He could taste the thrill. He could already imagine death draining from her bright eyes.

Blood pumped in his ears. Any minute now, her fear would rush into his veins. Mere seconds from the high, the relief, the bliss, Edward brought his hands to her throat. As he prepared for her eyes to fade, Caitlyn laughed.

The crashing sound was massive, and the room fell as silent as death.

"My neck is ticklish," she said, still squirming.

As if he hadn't seen Caitlyn until this second, Edward realized that his hands were on her throat.

"Oh, my God." Without hesitation, Edward dropped his arms and backed off.

"I'm sorry." Caitlyn blushed. "I ruined a good kiss, huh?"

"No . . . no. Not at all." Edward tried to regain his composure, but his thoughts slammed.

The Darkness enveloped him like black saran wrap. It bit into his neck. Stung his eyes. Swiped at his breath. "I felt dizzy for a moment."

"Are you okay?"

"Not feeling so good."

The Darkness howled.

"I should go home." Edward's voice trembled.

"I don't want you driving,"

"It's okay." The only thing he could think of, the only thing that meant anything was to get out of Caitlyn's house. *Now.*

The Darkness' insistence overwhelmed him. Like a panther, it paced inside his psyche. Its eyes, hollow. Its heart, vacant. The clock slashed the silence with every tick. With every tock.

"Can I help you?" Caitlyn offered. "Tell me what's happening, Edward. I'm a nurse. This is what I do."

The Darkness rebounded, and Edward's psyche bloomed like deadly oleander. The impulse—the need to kill for the sexual release, for the sheer pleasure of the after-kill glow—flooded him.

Edward tried to dull the uproar by downing another shot of Johnnie Blue. Losing control—the urge to kill too strong to defeat—he gulped two more swigs from the bottle.

Her death would be sweet.

"Gotta run." Sweat dripped from his brow. Edward fled to the door and opened it. It took everything he had to stay focused.

"Are you in pain, Edward? It's better to relax until we know—"

Her perfume intoxicated him.

Fucking do it, The Darkness sniped.

Edward turned and raced to his car.

"Edward, wait," Caitlyn yelled from the porch.

"I'll call you." Edward slammed the car door, screeched out of her driveway, and roared down the street.

CHAPTER 6

DESPERATE, EDWARD STOPPED at a liquor store and bought another bottle of scotch. Sitting in his car, sucking down a few gulps at a time, he watched a woman walk out of the liquor store and turn onto a secluded street.

The Darkness sat on Edward's shoulder and watched her too.

You've got to back off Caitlyn.

I've got my needs, the menace replied.

Fucking stay away from her. You know why she's important. Don't mess with me on this."

Waa, waa. The creature mimicked a baby's cry.

Edward pushed the shadow off his shoulder and onto the passenger seat. He turned to grab it, but The Darkness flew up to Edward's face and pecked hard.

You think you can control me?" The Darkness hissed. *I'm your best friend or your worst enemy. Your choice."*

Defeated, Edward glanced out the car window. The full moon hid behind a cloud like a sniper poised for the shot. He started the car, drove out of the parking lot, and turned the opposite direction.

I'll hunt anyone, anytime, Edward said. *Just leave Caitlyn out of this.*

How about the woman? The Darkness replied.

Which? At the cash register?"

The one who just left the liquor store.

Grab her off a neighborhood street? Edward shot back. *A little risky. Let's find someone—*

Her, the creature demanded.

No, too dangerous, Edward muttered.

I'll hunt anyone, The Darkness mocked.

Jesus. Okay. Yes

Edward turned onto the next street, zigzagged through the neighborhood, and parked. After getting out of his car, he jogged through backyards until he reached the dimly lit street where the woman from the liquor store still walked. Old trees gathered around houses like onlookers at a crime scene. The street lights hummed in the fog.

Was that a cop car?

Keeping his head down, Edward glanced at his Rolex to make it harder for a cruiser to see his features. *But why take a chance? One cop sees a man strolling down a deserted street—a woman walking ahead of him—the cop's going notice. Maybe even make a note about it. Medium-built man, dark hair, tall—maybe six feet.*

Then, they'd find the body. Shit, if I grab her, what the fuck am I going to do with the body? Leave her? Just dump her in the bushes? Doesn't seem proper. It's so much easier plucking them off the highway. They're on an adventure, and so am I.

But Edward had made a deal with The Darkness who'd kept its promise— not without some minor aggravation— and had resisted Caitlyn most of the day.

This is my chance. She's close to the bushes, close to her death. Edward increased his pace. *One push and she's down. She's asking for it. Walking alone.*

She was seconds from the shrubs. Edward shifted to a run. Closer. A few feet behind her. He shoved her between the bushes, flipped her onto her back, and tightened his hands around her neck.

The moon broke from the clouds and took aim. Lucky for Edward, he could see her eyes.

She kicked frantically.

"If you shut up, I won't hurt you."

The terror dulled her green irises, which sent a madness through Edward. Sound escaped his crooked mouth in low snarls. But then, she twisted like a wrestler and kneed him in the groin.

Fucking bitch.

He could barely move.

She pulled herself up and ran—screaming like the star of a low-budget horror flick. Edward peeked through the bushes. No one in sight. A few porch lights came on and turned off just as fast. Then nothing. Edward got up, scanned the street, and took off. The Darkness flew along for the ride— flapping its wings, screeching into the night. Through backyards and into a stand of trees, Edward stopped, gasping for breath.

Breathe.

The moon made peace with the night sky, and a brittle light streamed through the branches.

WELL, THAT WAS a fucking success, The Darkness scowled.

This is your fault. You goddamn provoke me. You push, even when the timing is off. Even if it's the worst possible location. Like tonight. Like fucking tonight. And now, this bitch has seen my face.

Nothing's stopping you now, The Darkness clucked. "Go take care of her."

She's probably home by now and has called the cops. Haven't you an ounce of sense?

Well, I, for one, am not satisfied. Click-clack. Click-clack. Click-clack. Better find someone fast, The Dark creature threatened.

Shit, we better get the hell out of here before the cops show. Edward's words were hot. Rushed.

With that, they raced to the car and headed to Aurora Avenue, where the prostitutes were easy prey.

CHAPTER 7

A KNOCKED AT Cate's front door. Then another.

"Hey," Cate said, opening the door to Edward. "What a nice surprise. I thought you'd already left."

"I couldn't go to Vegas without seeing you." He stepped over the threshold and nodded at Ruby, who sat in the chair closest to the fireplace. She wore gold lamé cropped pants and a cherry-red, lightweight cardigan. Large hoop earrings touched her shoulders, and a pair of thick false lashes looked like small awnings above her eyes.

"This must be the infamous Edward," Ruby said as she wiggled her way across the room to greet him. She offered her outstretched hand palm down for a proper greeting.

Edward obliged with a kiss on the back of her hand. "*Ma chérie.*" His smile was a charmer.

Ruby studied his blue-hydrangea eyes. Dreamy. She could almost fall into them. But something behind the eyes left her staring at him a pinch too long. Black specks floated inside the dark-rimmed irises like miniature sharks. An interesting juxtaposition—the heavenly blue littered with darkness. Unnoticeable if she'd hadn't been so close.

"Ruby, this is Edward. I'm so glad you two are finally meeting."

"The pleasure is mine. So, there really is a Ruby." Edward chuckled.

"I wondered the same about you." Ruby forced a smile. She wanted to be as captivated as Cate had been by this all-American, easy-on-the-eyes, well-put-together man. But it was too late. His perfect smile made her uneasy. He reminded her of a cartoon she'd seen in an issue of *Psychology Today.* In a swanky restaurant, two sheep sat at a table—except one of them was a fierce wolf hidden behind a sheep mask.

"Come in. Come in." Cate ushered them both into the living room.

"Ruby," Edward said as he touched the small of her back. "Cate didn't mention you were so attractive."

Ruby made her way to her chair, puffed up her bubble-shaped hairstyle with her hands, and pulled lipstick from her purse. *He better not hurt her,*

Ruby thought as she put on enough lipstick to make up fifteen beauty queens. His smooth demeanor hid a man with a cheating heart. She was sure of it.

"So, Cate tells me you're an attorney," Ruby said. "Forfeiture, right?"

"Yeah, I help people get their property back."

"You mean, you help *criminals* get their property back," Ruby corrected. "You do a lot of business in Las Vegas. That must be tricky keeping track of the laws in both states."

"That's what paralegals are for." His smile, devastating.

"Don't let him fool you." Cate glanced at Ruby. "Edward's a member of Mensa. His mind is a library."

"Impressive," Ruby said.

"Homemade lemonade?" Caitlyn stood up. "Edward?"

Nothing.

"Edward, lemonade?"

Edward tapped his heel. "No." *Tap. Tap. Tap.* "No, thanks."

"Why Las Vegas?" Ruby asked.

"I moved there and opened my practice after law school. Kept my office and my clients even though I moved back to Seattle."

"Got a girlfriend there, too?" She winked as if it were a big, fat joke.

"I did, about two years ago, but she's dead to me now." *Tap. Tap. Tap.* His heel pumped up and down. He glanced at his watch. "Damn, I've got to get on the road."

Ruby couldn't help but notice the edge in Edward's voice. When she glanced at him, he seemed to be glaring at her—his blue eyes now muddy and dim. He made her nervous. Refusing to let him see her anxiety, she batted her eyelashes as if they were handheld fans of plumage. "Oh, I wish you could stay." She was certain her smile hid her lie.

"Want lemonade or a shot of Johnnie Blue for the road?" Caitlyn offered as she turned to the kitchen.

"Yeah, a shot sounds superb." Edward stood, his hands in fists, and stared at the corner of the ceiling. "Never mind," he muttered, his voice now strained. "I'm going to hit the road."

"Oh, Edward." Cate turned back for a hug, but he'd already opened the door and headed for his car.

"Well, that was weird." Ruby watched him back out of the driveway and screech down the street. "I don't like the guy."

"He must be having a tough day. He gets antsy sometimes, that's all."

"Edward doesn't like me either." Ruby watched Cate plop onto the couch across from her.

"That's not true at all."

"He glared at me like he hated me."

"That's your imagination, Ruby."

"The conversation was *shvach*. My questions aggravated him." Ruby puffed her hair again. "I'll bet he doesn't like sharing you."

"He's a private person, and I'm sure he expected me to be alone."

"He does have a nice *tuchus*." Ruby pulled out her nail file.

"He's hot, right?" Cate laughed.

"Hot man, cold heart," She said as she shaped a nail.

"Oh, for heaven's sake, Ruby. You hardly spoke to him."

"He's got lying eyes. Like my Frank."

"Frank was a ladies' man. Besides, I'm not sure a woman who's been married four times is a great judge of character."

"Well, you might be right there." Ruby laughed.

CHAPTER 8

THREE BOYS RIDING their bikes along the Duwamish River in the industrial area of Seattle discovered the body. Within minutes of their call to 911, two beat cops eating pastries close to the area were the first to arrive. One cordoned off the scene while his partner talked to the boys.

When Detective Will Cambrey arrived, The Medical Examiner was already with the body. Will ducked under the yellow tape and headed toward the victim. Shaved head, five-foot-ten, Cambrey looked like a short Mr. Clean with brown eyes. He was no *GQ* cover guy, but good looking all the same. Masculinity oozed from him.

Until he'd moved to Seattle several years before, Will had spent a year in New Orleans, but he was born and raised in a Canton, Georgia. He dripped Southern charm, and when he spoke, his words were as sweet as mint julep syrup.

Will kept quiet about his initial deductions at a crime scene. The twitch in his right eye meant he was onto something. Oddly enough, when he sensed a lie, his left eye did the same.

"Whatcha got here?" Cambrey squatted next to Medical Examiner.

M.E. Rick Owens was a squirrel of a man with thick glasses and a combed-over part close to his left ear. The guy looked like a wiry Trump, which always gave Cambrey a laugh.

"Looks like we gotta organized killer. No signs of a struggle. No footprints. Nope, nothing," one detective said as he approached Cambrey. "Crime was committed somewhere else and dumped here."

"Jesus," Will muttered. Even after twelve years of being a cop, seeing a dead victim of violent crime still bothered him.

"Probably been here about a month." Owens pushed his sliding glasses back to the bridge of his nose. "Probable cause of death, strangulation."

"She's dressed like a hooker from Aurora," Will offered.

"Fuck," Medical Examiner Owens groaned.

"What?"

"Check out the ribbon around her neck." Owens lifted the lace with his pen. "We got a copycat?"

"Aw, shit," Will said, his Southern accent made his words blur together in a sing-song way. "I hope we don't find any more bodies."

A FEW WEEKS later, an environmental consultant walking along the bank of the Green River in Kent County noticed what he thought was a large, dead animal close to the river. Later identified as Cynthia Langford, the body had a lace ribbon tied around her neck. Cause of death, strangulation. She'd been dead a few weeks.

In the brush and close to her, pieces of a woman's skeleton were found with a lace ribbon torn and bloody near the skull.

The headlines roared, LACE RIBBON COPYCAT CLAIMS THREE IN SEATTLE AREA. With recollections of the terror that the original Lace Killer had evoked, Washington residents felt the darkness of death creeping back into their counties, their cities, their homes. Fewer kids walked home from school, hikers and joggers hit the gyms instead, and doors were dead-bolted.

Then nothing.

Two months passed. With no new bodies, a lightweight hope floated above Seattle like cirrus clouds. Perhaps the killer had moved on? At least, that's what the optimists thought until a hiker in the Snoqualmie Pass area stumbled across the body of a woman. A lace ribbon around her neck.

Edward had no interest in publicity, but now that newspapers, TVs, and the internet were abuzz with his work, well, it was difficult to say he didn't like the exposure. Flattered? Oh, yes, he was.

SEATTLE POLICE DEPARTMENT'S Downtown Captain Selma Thorten, a handsome woman with a chiseled face, wore a crow-colored jacket with a starched-white, ruffle-collared blouse. She stood at the head of the table.

The M.E., homicide detectives, special agents sat at the table. Watch commanders stood at the back of the room to gather information to brief officers at roll call for each shift.

First, a formal introduction, then Captain Thorten summarized the events leading up to the meeting. A whiteboard positioned behind Thorten showed a map of dumpsites with pictures of the victims and family photos of those who had been identified.

After the watch commanders were dismissed from the meeting, the detectives and FBI agents remained in the conference room for hours. They combed through files, compared crime scene photos, and discussed the similarities and differences between each murder.

Outside the Seattle Police Department, camped behind camera crews, citizens carried placards: "Protect Our Women Now," and "Stop the Copycat Killer." Everyone waited for a statement.

Armed with enough information, FBI Special Agent Lars Mills stepped out of the building to address the press. "This morning, a profile was established for the Copycat Killer. First, the Lace Ribbon Killer, Patrick Derry, strangled his victims and tied a lace ribbon around their necks before dumping them. He was executed twelve years ago.

"The Copycat Killer has committed similar crimes, including the lace ribbon around the neck of the bodies. Patrick Derry was an opportunist. So is the Copycat. This means he chooses his victims because the opportunity presents itself."

He nodded to Captain Thorten, who stepped close to the microphone.

"Women must be cautious—avoid walking alone, keep your doors locked, and stay alert," Thorten said. "We're asking citizens to be vigilant and to inform us of suspicious activity. Don't assume that this killer is some crazed-looking guy with an ax. He could be anyone. He blends in. Hides in plain sight."

Thorten motioned to the man at her side. "This is Lead Detective James Moran."

Moran stepped in front of the microphone. "We consider the Copycat to be extremely dangerous. Anyone who's witnessed anything suspicious, please contact us on our public tip line."

Questions sparked from reporters.

"How many more bodies have been found?" a young man shouted.

"I'm sorry, I can't reveal that information at the current time."

"Do you have any suspects?" another reporter called out.

"Investigations like this take time and tips," Moran replied. "The missing piece could be something any of our citizens could know. We need people to come forward no matter how insignificant they think their information is. I want to emphasize that no piece of information is too small to explore. Small tips help fill the holes and will bring this case together."

"Somebody knows who this is," Thorten said, stepping in front of the microphone. "Someone was privy to a conversation, whether it was firsthand or secondhand; somebody heard, saw, or knows something. It's crucial you contact us."

Both Mills and Thorten answered a few more questions and then headed back into the building. Reporters were still shouting questions as the headquarter doors closed.

CHAPTER 9

HE'D PULLED HER into the bushes. Tried to strangle her. Banged her head against the ground. Thank God her aim was good when she kicked him in the balls. Could she describe him? She tried to conjure a clear picture of him, but it was hazy. Height? Taller. Hair? Dark. Weight? Average. Face? Good-looking. Distinguishing features—a strong cologne she couldn't name.

To avoid updates about the Copycat Killer, Jennifer Cannon no longer watched the evening news. She skipped over the front page of the paper, and whenever a news update broke into her programs, she turned off the sound. But when she'd clicked on the TV that afternoon, investigators were calling for witnesses in the Copycat Killer murders.

All *she* could do was rush to the toilet and dry heave. Could her attacker have been the Copycat Killer? On the bathroom floor, Jennifer sobbed until, at last, she fell into exhaustion.

No matter what she did, she could not escape her thoughts. How brainless she'd been to walk alone after dark. What could she have been thinking? She thought of her parents, her friends, the public-at-large scrutinizing her. *Did you think a nice girl would take a stroll in the dark?* she imagined her father saying. And how could she answer? *I wanted a pack of cigs? It was only a couple of blocks away?*

"With all the news about the Copycat Killer, *you* walk down a dark street? Did I raise an imbecile?"

Jennifer tried to quiet the ruckus in her head. Between her father's accusations, her mother's tears, and judgment by her peers, it seemed like an impossible situation. Frozen by her anxiety, she said nothing.

She knew she should call the tip hotline, but they'd want more: a statement, sit with a sketch artist, speak out publicly. These were *not* viable options. What if he discovered she talked? Would *she* be found a few days later, on the bank of the Duwamish or the Green River?

Jennifer's guilt pounded her. *If they find another body, you'll be responsible,* the voices in her head yelled.

Torn, Jennifer picked up the phone but slammed it back down. Too disheartened to do much of anything since the attack, she preferred to stay close to home. She took a six-week medical leave of absence from her job as an administrative assistant at Amazon. Her doors had new locks, her windows had stoppers, and she had a new Smith & Wesson M&P M2.0 Pistol she kept by her bed—just in case.

CHAPTER 10

ALTHOUGH THE POLICE received many tips, nothing panned out. A few days after the press conference, frustrated detectives spent the morning in a conference room, brainstorming.

"A white male. In his thirties." FBI Agent Mills said. A twenty-five-year veteran profiler and investigator, he was a disheveled man in a tired sport coat and should-have-been-thrown-out-last-year pants. His head, shaved in a buzz cut, put emphasis on his gray mustache and deeply etched face. Clearly, he'd seen his share of violence.

Cambrey cut in. "He's dragging or carrying the bodies down to the riverbank. He's strong. Works out."

"We think carried. There were no drag marks," Lead Detective Moran advised.

"Local?" Captain Thorten inquired.

"We believe so. He's comfortable. I suspect he'll step-up his crimes. Out of the blue, these bodies show up once a month. The recovery period seems to be narrowing," Agent Mills replied. "Doesn't hold a steady job."

"Could be a student," Cambrey offered. "Someone must know something."

"If only a lead would come in." Thorten stood up from the round table and stretched. "I'll see if we can get some money to offer a reward—it's worth it to invest in the safety of the citizens."

Within a few days, the headline hit the press: $25,000 REWARD FOR INFORMATION LEADING TO THE ARREST OF THE PERSON RESPONSIBLE FOR THE COPYCAT KILLINGS. Another press conference. Mills was at the mic. "At the current time, we have no definite leads. We're hoping the reward will motivate someone to step forward."

"Do you think he leaves the bodies for someone to find?" a reporter asked.

"It appears so," Mills replied.

"We increased our patrols in all areas and ask that anyone who sees anything suspicious to please call the tip line or 911," Captain Thorten added.

When the press conference ended, Mills, Thorten, Moran, Cambrey, and partner LaKeisha Taylor returned to the conference room to discuss leads and investigation ideas.

CHAPTER 11

MAYBE SHE WAS safe, but Jennifer couldn't be sure. *Her attacker may not have been the Copycat Killer. Then what? Could this guy be hanging around town? Watching for her?*

It didn't matter who the attacker was. She realized that the longer she withheld information from the police, the more likely the assaults would continue. *How many other women locked themselves in their house wrapped in a blanket of fear? Who else had escaped and lived a scarred life?*

Her conscience gnawed at her. As much as she didn't want to admit it, the right thing—the only thing, really—was to contact the police.

It was a tough decision to be vulnerable. Her fear of being hunted and murdered immobilized her, and yet, she now understood there was no choice. If she didn't come forward, who would? She might be the only one who had escaped. She could save someone's life. Maybe more than one woman would be safer because of her.

It was painful, but she pushed herself forward and called the Seattle Police Department tip line.

"Yes, hello. I'm not sure how this works. I have information about . . . he tried to strangle me . . . I'm afraid if I tell, I'll be forced to be on the news, or my name will become public." Jennifer's words collapsed into each other.

"Whoa, whoa—slow down," the detective said.

Although Jennifer paused, the pounding of her heart smashed on.

"Okay, now. You have information?"

"Well, I'm not sure. A few weeks ago, I was walking home . . . a guy tried to strangle me." Making a complete mess of it, Jennifer fought the sudden urge to hang up.

"Can you describe him?"

Jennifer did her best.

"Okay, can you hold for a sec?" the detective asked.

Will Cambrey came into the room just as the detective stood.

"Anything interesting?" Will tossed his jacket across his chair.

"I think we got a hit. She's on the phone now."

"Cambrey," Will said after grabbing the phone. He listened then said, "Look, I'm fixin' to protect your identity, would you come downtown for a spell? You might just know something that could save women's lives."

Cambrey didn't want to jinx anything. Even so, the urge to jump up on his desk and yell through a bullhorn, "Y'all, we have a witness!" pumped up his adrenaline.

"I'm afraid to leave my apartment."

"Look, now, I'll come to you, pick you up, bring you to the station, and take you home."

"I don't know," Jennifer said. "Let me think about it—"

"Every minute counts." Will tried to keep his tone calm. "This guy could be the Copycat Killer. Either way, he's dangerous, ma'am. The sooner we get your information, the sooner—"

"Okay, but can a woman come with you?"

"Of course." Cambrey wrote down Jennifer's name, phone number, and address. "We're on our way."

Before he left, jinx or no jinx, Cambrey climbed onto his desk and yelled, "I'm as happy as a tick on a fat dog!"

IT TOOK CAMBREY and partner, LaKeisha Taylor twenty minutes to get to Jennifer's apartment. After making them hold their IDs to the peephole. She unlocked the deadbolts, but the still-fastened sliding chain allowed her to creak the door open a few inches. Again, she had them show their IDs so she could read them. Satisfied, she unfastened the lock and let the officers in.

The moment LaKeisha came through the door, Jennifer ran to her and hugged her. "I've been so alone. I've needed a woman to talk to but couldn't call my mother or my sisters. My family wouldn't understand."

"It's okay, sweetie," LaKeisha said, patting Jennifer's back.

Instead of pulling from the hug, Jennifer plunged into sobs. LaKeisha walked her to the couch and sat with her.

"I don't know how to move past this. I don't want to go to the police station."

"Why don't you tell us what you remember?

"My mind is blank. I can't remember anything." Jennifer was starting to hyperventilate.

"Slow down, sweetie. Take easy breaths. We're here for you," LaKeisha murmured.

"I . . . can't . . . even . . ."

"Take a long, slow breath, Jennifer," LaKeisha said, her voice calm.

"I can't . . . can't breathe . . ."

"Slow, sweetie. A long breath."

Jennifer tried to breathe. Hesitated. Then exhaled.

"There you are," LaKeisha said, her tone compassionate. "Keep breathing like that. Long inhales." She patted Jennifer's arm. "You might find you're more comfortable at the station. Sometimes a different environment helps."

Jennifer's breathing had now changed from fast, short puffs to long inhalations and exhalations.

"I'll set you up with the Victim Support Services. Plus, Harborview Medical Center has traumatic stress counseling. And there are more resources we can discuss after we have our talk."

THE FACTS GATHERED from Jennifer gave the profilers an assortment of clues. His appearance? Dark-colored hair, long on top and cut short on sides. He seemed taller than Jennifer. Toned. Clean-cut. "He wore a cologne I've never smelled before."

"Reckon you'd recognize it if you smelled it again?"

"Yes, it was very distinctive."

"And you've never smelled it before that night?"

Jennifer shook her head.

Jennifer spent time with the sketch artist, and after many tries, they came up with a composite. *Did it look like him?* She wasn't sure. It was dark that night, and the assault was fast. *But, yes. Maybe. Thin lips. Medium, nondescript nose. Dead eyes.*

CHAPTER 12

EDWARD TOSSED AND turned. His mind flashed on images of Caitlyn. She screams as he smashes her with a hammer to shut her up, she struggles as he strangles her, he sees the light fading from her tropical-blue eyes. He tried to replace these visions with thoughts of their good times together, but the damn pictures kept coming.

He felt drugged, groggy, yet tightly wound. This was his first major conflict with The Darkness. Until now, they'd had a symbiotic relationship. The Darkness had free rein to feed its craving, and in return, it would leave Caitlyn alone. A deal where they both reaped the rewards.

But lately, the entity wanted more. And sure, it was a burden to keep up with the beast's needs, but it was doable.

But why Caitlyn?

Caitlyn and Edward had been dating for three months. They watched romantic movies, walked at Green Lake, read Neruda's poetry, searched for rare flowers, dressed up for symphony nights, and shared long conversations. But most of the time, in the background, he struggled with the evil spirit that owned his soul.

What would it be like to kill Derry's daughter?

He grabbed his forehead. It felt as if his skull would crack. He was upside down and inside out. Twisted and confused. Caitlyn was his most precious trophy. His idol's daughter and now Edward's girl. Kill her? What the hell was he thinking?

To appease The Darkness and to protect his Caitlyn, Edward prowled regularly. He'd take road trips for the day out of Seattle and do his damage in new parts of the state. He did whatever it took to seduce that insidious demon away from Caitlyn's delicate neck.

CATE WAS OBLIVIOUS to Edward's inner struggle. New to relationships, unaccustomed to having a steady guy, she paid little attention to the discrepancies in Edward's stories. He arrived late for dates or left abruptly;

sometimes, he was antsy, sometimes not. She chalked up the amount he drank to stress.

Cate had pressures too. Her work schedule had tightened and kept her ragged. Another unexplained death had occurred at the hospital. In situations such as these, some hospitals kept tight-lipped—the administration wanted to avoid lawsuits, police inquiries, and bad publicity. If an internal investigation occurred, the suspected violator would be asked to leave, regardless of the outcome. Simple as that.

Not that anyone was a suspect in the sudden downward trend in the health of a few critical care cases, but the hospital staff was on alert for foul play when a recovering patient took a sudden nosedive and died.

One evening, after barbequing steaks at Edward's home, Cate leaned back in her patio chair and sighed.

"We're getting a Pyxis," she groaned.

"Nice," Edward replied, not looking up from the newspaper.

"No," Cate blurted. "Not nice at all."

"What's wrong?"

"The hospital. They're getting a Pyxis."

"Meaning?" Edward tried to sculpt the edginess he felt.

"When I need meds for a patient, I'll have to go through an automated dispensing machine. It's a pain. Another hurdle to jump. I'm getting to like this hospital less and less."

Without saying another word, Edward lifted Cate from her chair, carried her over to the pool, and dropped her into the water.

"Fudge," Cate yelled once she surfaced. "What the heck was that for?"

"Got your mind off your problems, right?" Edward winked.

"Very funny," she said with a pout.

He helped her out of the pool, wrapped her in a towel, and hugged her. "Hey." He smiled. "What do you call a pig that does karate?"

Cate shrugged.

"A pork chop."

Cate couldn't help but laugh.

CATE CHANGED OUT of her wet outfit and put on one of Edward's t-shirts and a pair of his drawstring yoga pants. In the master bathroom, she peered into the full-length mirror and bowed her head. She used to wear her dad's pajama tops. He'd lift her high and twirl, saying, "Who's the airplane?"

"I am, Daddy. I am."

Then he'd whoosh her across the room, her arms out like wings.

Tears welled in Cate's eyes. Maybe part of her dad's need to kill came from hatred of her mother? The cold-hearted be-ach. Cate shook her head. Her mother blamed Cate for her sister's death. It wasn't fair.

Unable to resist a ringing phone, Cate's mother had told the five-year-old to watch her two-year-old sister, Maddie, who was taking a bath. Maddie played mermaid and laid face down in the water. Then she pushed herself up and down like a fish. As for Cate, all was well. When her mother came back and turned Maddie face up, her lips were blue.

"Oh my God, Caitlyn. Oh my God! You killed Maddie!"

Cate slammed back to her reflection in the mirror.

Daddy said that it wasn't my fault. He yelled and said that Mother shouldn't have left Maddie and me alone. God, I miss Daddy.

"WELL, DON'T YOU look adorable?" Edward stepped behind Caitlyn and embraced her. In the mirror's reflection, they looked like longtime lovers. "I like you in my clothes."

"Edward?"

"Yes." He kissed her neck.

"Have you ever seen a dead person?"

Edward's reflected image showed his face blanch and his blue eyes fade to a murky gray. He turned Caitlyn to face him. "Where'd that come from?"

Caitlyn walked over to the bed, sat down, and fell into tears.

"You want to tell me?" Edward sat next to her and held her in his arms.

"I was watching my baby sister for my mother. Maddie was in the tub. I was only five. I didn't understand what drowning was."

"Of course, you didn't."

"Mother said it was my fault. That I killed Maddie to have Daddy all to myself."

"It was your mother's fault," Edward said, his voice low but sharp.

"That's what Daddy said."

"Great minds think alike." Edward thought about his hero and how much Caitlyn had loved him. Loved him still. And Edward could see why.

"I've never told anyone. Not even Ruby. Do you think I'm horrible?"

"Absolutely not. I wish I could be more like that."

"Like what?"

"Like how you just opened up to me." Edward didn't know where the fuck that came from, but it seemed to be the right thing to say.

Caitlyn looked at him and smiled.

Even so, Edward sensed a darkness slithering into the room. On his dresser sat his nemesis grinding its teeth. A sudden desire to rid himself of Caitlyn poured over him like gasoline. One tiny spark and he'd turn into a fireball of death. He started to pace. "I don't know about you, but I sure could use a shot of Johnnie Blue." He took Caitlyn's hand and walked to the wet bar. The shot calmed The Darkness. This time.

CHAPTER 13

A SKETCH OF the assailant was now in most of the surrounding area's newspapers, and tip-line calls were stacking up. Unfortunately, the leads went nowhere.

Cate and a co-worker had a good laugh when another nurse brought in *The Seattle Times.* "This sketch sort of looks like your boyfriend." The other nurse chuckled.

And it *was* funny. A nice, wealthy, handsome guy like Edward didn't need to attack women—almost any woman would want to have sex with a guy like him. Even so, the floor nurses teased Cate about her boyfriend.

Edward took Cate to lunch often and got to meet "the girls" and Nurse Scott Snider. Occasionally, Edward sent flowers with a note for the nurses. He brought bagels and cream cheese. Croissants and Cookies. It was almost as if he were wooing the entire Critical Care staff.

And oh, did they love it. Edward's charisma drew women (and Scott, for that matter) to him. When he stopped in, everyone lit up. He was like a lantern in an otherwise barren night—what with the pressure on everyone, what with the whispers and rumors, and that darn Pyxis.

Getting meds to patients put the staff on overload. Already backed up with doctors' requests and working under the scrutiny of Supervisor Nurse Sarah Bloom, each nurse carried her own burden. Plus, a temperamental machine, the Pyxis required regular on-site tech support.

Perhaps something distracted Supervisor Sarah Bloom the night she went missing. She carried pepper spray in her pocket each time she made the trek from the medical center to her car in the parking garage. When Sarah didn't show up for her shift, the staff knew something was wrong. She'd had never missed a day of work. Not once in the ten years she'd been at Harborview Medical Center.

Edward had been in the parking garage the night Sarah disappeared. He saw her approaching and leaned against the door of his car.

Watching.

Sarah passed him—how fortunate for Edward. What a shame for Sarah Bloom.

See what I mean, Edward said to The Darkness. *They come to me if I just let nature take its course.* Edward crept behind Sarah and tapped her shoulder.

Sarah spun to face him.

"Oh my God, it's you, Edward." She let out a sigh of relief. "You scared the crap out of me, I thought you were the Copycat Killer." Her voice trembled.

"A lot of good your pepper spray did," Edward said with a smile.

"How did you know about that? Cate?"

"Speaking of Caitlyn, I've got something I'd like your opinion on."

And sure, she would look at the present he'd bought for Caitlyn. As they walked back to his car, Edward scanned the area, opened the trunk, hit her head with the hammer, threw her in, and shut the trunk.

"Not to worry," he said to the unconscious Sarah. "You'll be safe here alone with your pepper spray."

Both he and The Darkness laughed.

When Edward walked into the nurses' lounge, he had an armful of treats. Scott and the girls were thrilled.

CHAPTER 14

HAVING BEEN A hotbed for serial killings over the years, the outlying counties and the city of Seattle wasted no time opening investigations of missing persons, including Sarah Bloom.

Will Cambrey stepped off the elevator on five-east with a pen behind his ear and tablet in hand. He approached each nurse with the same questions:

"Had Sarah acted any different?"

"Did she have a boyfriend?"

"Had she seemed depressed?"

"Had she said something that could have indicated there was a problem?"

Most of the staff was sure it was the Copycat Killer. Sarah had never made it to her car. She hadn't shown up for work the next day. And didn't call in.

Unless, as Cate overheard a few nurses whispering, Bloom was responsible for the deaths of those critical care patients. She *did* have access to all drugs. Perhaps she accidentally overdosed them? Or maybe, she had done it intentionally and was seconds away from being found out.

Had she rented a car?

Left the state?

Rumors ran amok. But as for the police, not one staff member offered any scenario other than the Copycat Killer took her. The police had no knowledge of the suspicious deaths, so the fact that Sarah Bloom may have been the perpetrator was not on their radar. Period.

"EXCUSE ME, MA'AM. Got a minute?" Will's Southern accent smoothed his words into a melody.

"I'm just leaving," the nurse replied.

"I'll make this fast." Will glanced out the hospital's waiting area's window at the cheerless, late afternoon sky then grabbed his pen. "I'm Detective Will Cambrey. Y'all stay busy up here." Will stretched the word "here" from one syllable to two—hee-ah.

The nurse shrugged.

"How well did you know Miss Bloom?"

"Just from work," she replied.

"And when was the last time you saw her?"

"Last night, around ten." The nurse glanced at her watch.

"Did she do or say anything unusual?" Will studied the nurse intently. She was attractive in a fresh-faced way. Her eye color resembled blue irises in bloom, and her smile could steal a man's heart.

She looked down at the floor. "Not unusual. She said goodnight, and she'd see me tomorrow."

"Other nurses say she carried pepper spray in her pocket. Did you know this?"

"Yeah. Sarah made a big deal about protecting ourselves, since, you know, the Copycat."

"Was Miss Bloom well-liked?" A wisp of the nurse's flowery perfume caught Will's attention.

"She was all right. Truth is . . ." She lowered her voice. "She was, you know, a real be-ach. She was on us a lot."

"A be-ach?"

"I don't swear."

Well, bless her heart, Will thought. *A real lady.*

"Did she pick on anyone in particular?" Will scribbled something on his tablet.

"She micro-managed us all."

"Did you look out to the parking garages that night?"

"In my spare time?" The nurse laughed. "No."

"Have you seen anyone suspicious hanging 'round the hospital?"

"Half the people here are suspicious." The nurse chuckled.

"Sorry, ma'am, I didn't catch your name."

She hesitated. "Look, I've got to run."

"Okay, Ms. . . .?"

"Give me just a sec. Let me drop this off." The nurse nodded to the charts she was carrying and disappeared around the corner.

CATE TUCKED HERSELF into the alcove and took a moment to breathe. Sudden anxiety screeched through her. If she said her name, would the officer know her father was Patrick Derry? Would he tell everyone? Cate dropped the charts off at the nursing station and walked back to the detective.

"I'm Cate Derry."

"Derry, huh?"

She forced a smile. *Did he know?*

The officer handed Cate his card. "You call me, right?" Will tucked the pen behind his ear. She noticed his face flush. "I mean if you remember anything else."

"Sure."

"GUESS WHO SHOWED up at the hospital tonight?" Cate said as she walked through Edward's doorway.

"I don't know. Who?"

Cate laid her jacket on the dark leather couch, sat a bag of groceries on the coffee table, and crossed the room to hug him.

"The police. They asked questions about Sarah. Like maybe she ran away or had a jealous boyfriend who did her in. That sort of stuff."

"From what I read, it sounds like the Copycat." Edward sat in his favorite plush leather chair and closed the book he'd been reading. "She's his type."

"His type?" Cate looked sharply at Edward. "How do you know he has a type?"

"Just read it right here." He pointed at *The Seattle Times* on the small table next to him. "He likes women in their twenties and thirties."

Cate gave Edward a light kiss on the cheek. "And meanwhile, everyone wonders if Sarah had anything to do with those critical care patients who died."

Edward took a sip of his scotch. "Ah . . . that's a good twist to the story. Angel of Death nurse murdered by a serial killer. *Qui ressemble s'assemble.*"

Cate laughed. "You and your French. What's it mean?"

"Birds of a feather, takes one to know one . . ."

Cate flopped down in a chair next to Edward. "What about me?" Cate unsnapped her barrettes and laid them on the coffee table.

"You, my dear, are gorgeous."

"I'm serious. *I'm* his type."

Edward took her hand. "From what I've read, he's an opportunist. Not so much a type—my guess. Those women were in the wrong place at the wrong time."

"I was afraid to leave tonight," she said. "Sarah always carried her pepper spray in her pocket. A lot of good that did."

"You've got to have that canister in your hand. Otherwise, you're screwed," Edward said, his tone flat.

"Everyone's afraid. Even Scott wanted someone to walk him to his car." Edward tried to contain his amusement.

"I'm buying a gun." Cate rubbed the back of her neck

"Hey, hey, hey," Edward blurted. He took Cate's hand, and together they walked to the couch. "The hospital should hire a security guard. If not, I will."

"You'd do that?"

"Of course, I would. That's what boyfriends do, right?"

CHAPTER 15

AFTER HE RETURNED to the station, Will searched until he found Patrick Derry's file. The mention of Derry's daughter was sparse. She was young when they came for her father. Her mother moved them to Tacoma after Derry's arrest and severed all contact with him. She applied to have their last name changed but never went through with it. The daughter, Caitlyn, graduated from high school with honors. She attended nursing school in Seattle and moved to Cincinnati for a job at Mercy Hospital. From there, she moved to Albuquerque, then Phoenix, and on, until finally landing at the Medical Center in Seattle.

"Well, butter my butt and call me a biscuit," Will muttered.

"What's up, Cambrey?" Mills said as he passed Will's desk.

"A nurse I spoke with today is Patrick Derry's daughter."

Mills stopped in his tracks. "*The* Patrick Derry? As in Lace-Ribbon-Killer Derry?"

"Yep, sure is." Will put the file back in order and dropped it on the corner of his desk.

"Do you think it's just a coincidence?"

"Well, Mills, might-could be. Sit a spell and look at these files. Meantime, I'm fixin' to have another chat with Miss Derry."

"I GOT A call from that police officer this morning." Cate twisted her watch around her wrist. "He's coming by at noon."

Ruby leaned back on Cate's couch; Pipsqueak nuzzled on her belly. After handing Ruby a glass of her homemade lemonade, Cate sat across from her.

"Hmm . . . The guy calls the next morning after he questions you at work? Girlfriend, men are just falling out of the sky." Ruby scratched Pipsqueak's belly. "Got any to spare; let me know."

"It's not like that. He has more questions."

"What? He's coming over 'cause you're a suspect?" Ruby laughed.

"I told you he'd figure out who my dad was. I hate the police. They're so darn nosy."

"He needed an excuse to see you again."

"Like I'd be interested in a cop!" Cate rubbed her arms and looked around the living room. "When I said my last name, I could see it in his eyes. He knew."

"Cate." Ruby sat up. "Just because you have the same last name doesn't mean everyone thinks you're related. Do you think everyone with the name Bundy is related to Ted?"

Yes, Cate thought.

"And even if the cop knew . . . what's the big deal?" Ruby added.

"Seattle's too darn small."

"Do you want me to be here when he comes?" Ruby took a sip of her lemonade. "I helped your mama through all this; I'm happy to help you."

"Yeah, maybe."

"Okay, I'll get these curlers out of my hair and put my face on." Ruby moved Pipsqueak to the couch and stood. "Be back soon."

Cate nodded and watched Ruby head to the front door.

Ruby stopped in the doorway and turned. "Want a couple of makeup hints?" she said with a wink and a chuckle. With that, she wiggled her way to her small home next door.

To relieve tension, Cate turned her head side to side. Stress tightened her neck muscles, and a nerve tingled in front of and behind her ear. *The great auricular nerve is alive and well.* Cate flashed on a chart naming the nerves of the head she'd memorized in nursing school. She massaged her temples, neck, and shoulders.

At least at work, the momentum was fast and nonstop. She could forget about things. She could blow off steam. Have a sense of control. When she had no distractions, her anxiety flared.

What if her fellow employees found out who her dad was, then what? Would she no longer be trusted? Would she lose her excellent standing in the temporary supervisor's eyes?

Within two hours, the officer was at Cate's door. Ruby had already returned and was perched in the easy chair and waiting for an introduction.

"Detective Camprey." Cate opened the door wider and stepped aside.

"Cambrey," Will corrected. "But, please, call me Will." He walked into Cate's living room. "Man, it's hot as all get-out!"

Cate motioned to Ruby. "This is my friend Ruby."

"Good afternoon, ma'am."

Ruby fluffed her brazen-red hair and gave Will a flirtatious smile. "Why, Detective, it sho' enough is hot as a lizard's tail on asphalt!" Ruby, who'd suddenly developed a Southern accent, offered her hand.

Cate shot her an I-want-him-out-of-here-as-soon-as-possible look.

"Can I get you some lemonade, Officer . . . I mean, Will," Ruby said as if ignoring Cate's silent reprimand.

"Well, I just might. Thank you, Ruby."

Ruby headed to the kitchen.

Cate motioned to the couch. "I've already told you everything I know."

As Will situated himself, Cate sat in her chair. Her mouth felt parched, and her eyes dry. She'd rather be anywhere but here.

"I know who your father was," Will offered quietly. "I'm hoping you could know something that might just shed some light on our boy, the Copycat." The words rolled off his tongue with a southern twist. He glanced toward the kitchen. "Reckon we should speak in private?"

Ruby came into the living room and handed Will a glass of lemonade.

"It's okay to talk in front of Ruby. She knows." Cate played with her watch. "But please, don't mention this to anyone at my work."

"This is between y'all and me," Will said and gave Cate a wink. He pulled out his pad and pen. "Now, I know this goes a long way back, but do you remember anyone that your father knew . . . quite a few years younger than your father . . . someone who wrote to him in prison or visited him before or during the prison years?"

"No," Cate said quickly. The sooner this was over, the better.

"Did your mother keep any of his belongings?"

"My mother had nothing to do with him once they caught him." *Darn, leave already.*

"Did y'all attend the execution? I'm sorry to dredge all this up—"

"No."

"Do you remember anything odd about your father?"

"Besides the fact he was a serial killer? No, I think that about sums it up." Cate snapped.

"I'm sorry, ma'am."

"Can I get you some cookies," Ruby cut in. "I brought a batch over." She rocked her hips side to side as she made her way to the kitchen, the door swinging behind her.

"How about I make this up to you over dinner," Will said.

A look came over Will's face that showed he was just as surprised as Cate that he'd asked her out.

"I'm seeing someone," Cate replied.

"Oh, I didn't . . . it's just that . . ."

"What if I cooked dinner for you both?" Ruby said as if she'd been listening from the kitchen. She placed a platter of home-baked *rugelach* on the coffee table. "I make a brisket you can cut with a butter knife. And chopped liver—the old-fashion way—with a grinder and *schmaltz*. Right, Cate?"

Cate shot Ruby a what-the-heck-are-you-doing look.

"But no police talk," Ruby said as if that would appease Cate.

Will glanced at Cate and caught her shrug.

"Well, I'd like nothing better than a home-cooked meal," Will replied. "Much appreciated."

"Hmph," Cate said, glaring at Ruby

WILL HAD ONLY been gone a few minutes when Ruby moved over to Cate's couch and started up.

"There's nothing wrong with playing a little hard to get." Ruby bit into her rugelach—one of her favorite pastries. "You could use a few friends."

"I'm used to time alone. I like it." Cate reached for another cookie. "Who wants a policeman for a friend, anyhow?"

"It's not like you have a cache of drugs in your closet." Ruby laughed. "And he's damn cute if you want my opinion."

"If you think he's so cute, invite him over by himself."

"Hon, the only way I'd get a man like him to my house is if there'd been a crime."

"Want me to break and enter?" Cate dangled her leg over the arm of her chair.

"Only if you guarantee a cop as cute as Will comes to the rescue. When's Edward due back?"

"Tomorrow." Cate put half the cookie back on the coffee table. "If I eat any more of these, I'll have to double my time at the gym."

"He sure is gone a lot, that one. What kind of lawyer did you say he is?"

"Something with forfeitures."

"You sure he's not playing around with anyone else?"

"What makes you ask that?"

"Usually, when two people see each other, it's hot and heavy in the beginning. Are you sleeping with him?"

"Ruby! Edward respects me. He wants us to build a strong relationship first."

"Men like Edward are interested in sex, doll face. If he's not doing it with you, you can damn well be sure he's doing it with someone else. When he goes to Vegas on 'business,' I'll bet there's *monkey* business involved." Ruby picked up the plate of goodies.

"He's got a big clientele there."

"Maybe he's got a girl there, too." Ruby disappeared into the kitchen. "I don't know what it is," she called to Cate, "but I'd keep my eyes open."

"No worries." Cate shrugged. "Edward's not only honest; he's loyal."

Ruby yawned. "Sounds like bubba maisa to me."

"When you get to know him better, you'll see what I mean."

"Sure thing," Ruby replied.

"Edward likes me. He'll like you too."

CHAPTER 16

"C'MON, IT'LL BE fun." Cate said to Ruby after pouring their morning cup of coffee.

"I don't know." Ruby stirred the sugar into her drink. "I don't think Edward cares for me."

"If he didn't, he wouldn't have invited you—he's the one that brought it up. He wants to get to know you better." Cate sat across from Ruby at the kitchen table and munched toast cut from the *challah* Ruby had baked. "It's supposed to be beautiful today. We can have a barbeque and sit by the pool.

"So, you didn't plant the idea?"

"I promise. He said he'd like to do a barbeque, and maybe you'd like to join us."

"Well, fancy that."

"I thought we'd hit the road around one. I have to be at work tonight, so Edward said he'll give you a ride home."

"Notice anything different?" Ruby batted her eyes.

"Oh, my gosh. Longer eyelashes. How did you get that size lash to stay on your eyes?"

"They're held on with magnets." Ruby pulled one off and showed Cate the tiny magnets on the lash band.

"What do the magnets hold on to?"

"Simple. Magnetic eyeliner." Ruby put the lash near the liner, and the eyelash popped on. She fluttered her lashes again. "Sexy."

SITTING ON HIS deck, Edward rested on a tightly woven chair while Cate and Ruby sat on the pool's edge and kicked water. "It's incredible here," Ruby said, taking in the surrounding forest.

"Lots of bugs today." Cate swatted at a passing fly that landed on the birdbath and then headed back to annoy her again. "Jeezle, Pete."

"God, Caitlyn." Edward laughed. "Where did you come up with that one? It's a hundred years old."

"I remember stuff," Cate replied.

"Oh!" Ruby screeched. A fat yellow jacket had landed on her wrist. "I'm allergic to bees." Her voice trembled.

"It's not a bee, it's a wasp," Edward said, his voice flat.

The wasp seemed content to walk up Ruby's arm toward her shoulder.

"Somebody get this thing off me, *now*."

"Just hold still," Edward said, "and don't show it you're afraid."

"Bubba Maisa. It couldn't care less if I'm frightened. It all depends on its mood." Ruby froze. "And I've never seen a wasp in a good mood."

"Bubba maisa?" Edward said. "What's that mean?"

"I'm serious. Someone get this thing off me before I panic."

"I don't want to get it angry," Caitlyn said.

"Okay, I'm diving in. One. Two—"

"Ruby, it will sting you before you hit the water," Edward warned. "Stay still. It's your only chance."

"The hell with this," Ruby yelled as she did a forward tumble into the pool. Just as she hit the water, the bee lifted and flew off. Ruby swam the length of the pool, popped out of the water, and said, "See, no bee." She held her arm up in the air and waved.

"Wasp," Edward said sharply. "You're lucky it didn't sting you. And anyway, I'm right." He closed the book he was reading. "You should have stayed still."

"But you saw me move and not get stung," Ruby said, lifting her chin and straightening her posture. "*I* was right."

"Sorry, the *wasp* was already gone."

"No matter. The proof is in the facts."

"The wasp flew away right before you moved. I'm certain." Edward said firmly. *Ruby is as stubborn as she is annoying.*

"Because you're *always* right." Ruby's tone was heavy with sarcasm.

"Why do bees have sticky hair?" Edward said, ignoring Ruby.

"I don't know. Why?" Caitlyn replied.

"Because they use honeycombs."

Caitlyn had a good laugh. Ruby just groaned.

"How about dinner?" Caitlyn suggested. She looked at a dripping-wet Ruby. "Oh dear, you're missing an eyelash."

Edward pointed to the lash floating close to where Caitlyn still sat.

"It looks like a caterpillar." She scooped the lash and handed it to Edward while Ruby climbed the ladder out of the pool. "I'm heading for the bathroom, be right back," Caitlyn said as she stood up.

"I'm going to slip out of my suit and put on my clothes," Ruby added.

Ruby seems miffed, Edward thought. *Good. The angrier she gets, the more friction between Ruby and Caitlyn.*

She reached for the lash in Edward's palm, but he grabbed her wrist. "I'd be careful if I were you," he muttered as he squeezed firmly. "Seems like those lashes pop off as easy as they pop on. They're not as secure as you think." He laughed and released his grip.

Ruby's wrist was red, and her eyes held a delicious fear. She plucked the lash from Edward and hurried to the French door.

"I put our bags on Edward's bed. Down the hall to the left," Caitlyn said.

"I'll be back soon." She hurried through the house to keep water from dripping everywhere.

ONCE IN EDWARD'S bedroom, Ruby changed into leopard pedal pushers, a black blouse that tied at the waist, rhinestone earrings, and two gold bracelets loaded with charms. As she ran her fingers through her hair, she realized she no longer had the eyelash in her hand. Ruby got on her hands and knees. Searching the brown carpet, she saw a driver's license. She reached between the bed and the nightstand and grabbed the card.

Ruby had suspected he'd been cheating all along. Now she had the proof in her hand. *Cynthia* . . . She wished she could see better without her glasses.

"We wondered what you were doing."

The demonic sound of Edward's voice caused Ruby to jerk her head up. She jammed the ID into her bra. *Had he seen her holding the license? Should she say something?* "I lost my lash," she said. A slight shakiness lined her words.

Edward had a smile on his face, but it seemed manufactured. The look in his cold, vacant eyes frightened her.

"I guess it's a lost cause." Ruby shrugged.

Edward stepped into the room. "How unfortunate for you." Even his voice sounded different. Deeper. Rougher. And he stood there, glaring at her . . . but not. He seemed focused on the wall behind her.

"Edward?" He seemed transfixed. Was he having some kind of seizure? "Are you okay?" Ruby asked, now standing.

"I will be soon . . ." Edward seemed to drop back into himself. He grasped Ruby by the hand. "Let's get a shot of Johnnie Blue."

"ANY WAY YOU could drop me off at home?" Ruby whispered to Caitlyn when she made it back to the pool.

Edward had stopped to grab another bottle of Johnnie Blue at his bar.

"Why are you whispering?" Caitlyn glanced at her watch. "God, I'll be late as it is. Edward doesn't mind."

"I'd hate for him to make that drive into town and back home again." Ruby's face felt stretched.

Edward's home, nestled in the trees, was spectacular, but the trip from Index to Caitlyn's house in Lynnwood took an hour. The thought of being alone with Edward for that long unnerved Ruby. She was almost certain he'd seen the driver's license, and she didn't want to have *that* conversation with him. He would ask her not to tell Caitlyn about the affair. Say it was a onetime thing. Promise her it was over.

Should she tell Cate? Stay out of it? Ruby had been in similar situations and knew the result was a no-win either way. If she tells Cate, there's the "shoot-the-messenger" outcome. If she doesn't, when Cate finds out—*and she will*—she'll feel as if Ruby had betrayed her.

"Edward?" Cate called.

"No, don't ask—" Ruby started.

"You sure you're up to taking Ruby home?"

"I'm looking forward to it." Edward came from the pool deck into the kitchen. "It'll give us time to get to know one another." He glanced at Ruby and smiled.

"I hate to make you go out of your way. I could get a ride to the hospital with Cate and Uber home. It's not that far."

Edward's eyes met Ruby's. "No, really. I insist."

CHAPTER 17

"SO, RUBY?" EDWARD said after ten minutes of dead silence. He kept his eyes on the road ahead but sensed Ruby's apprehension. "You want to tell me what you hid when I came into the bedroom?"

"A driver's license. I found it while looking for my lash. I didn't mean to pry."

"Why the hell did you put it in your bra?" he said with a strained laugh. He glanced at her.

"I didn't want you to think I was snooping. I knew if I put it under the bed after you left, you'd find it. But then you waited for me, and I kept it in my bra."

"Really? Did you see whose license it was?"

I didn't have my glasses so didn't see the name but . . . this whole thing is so embarrassing."

Ruby was a liability; she had to go. It took everything he had not to kill her at that moment.

Perched close to the rearview window, the monstrosity partially spread its wings. *Click-clack. I say we do it now, boss. You're still in the forest. Pull off and get the high.*

"No," Edward said out loud.

"I'm sorry. I didn't quite catch that," Ruby said.

"No reason to be embarrassed . . . And it's not what you think," Edward said.

"How do you know what I think?"

"I'm a member of Mensa."

"I'm impressed."

"I trust you, Ruby. You can trust me."

"Are you having an affair? I'm not surprised. I've suspected all along."

A tsunami of relief soaked through Edward. Ruby's suspicions lead her into an endless maze. "Ruby, Ruby, Ruby."

Oh, for fuck's sake, The Darkness snarled.

"And no, I'm not having an affair. I'm crazy about Cate."

"That's what I get be for being such a mother hen," Ruby replied.

"Where's the license now?"

"I put it back under your bed."

"I sure could use a shot of scotch. I'm going to pull over."

"*Oy vey ist mir*," Ruby said. "Are you going to drink and drive?"

"What the hell language are you speaking?"

"Yiddish."

"What's it mean?" Edward turned on to a dirt road that led into the forest.

"It means 'Oh no,'" Ruby replied.

"Oh no, what?"

"You driving drunk."

Edward pulled to the side of the road. "One swig does not mean drunk." He climbed out of the car, opened the trunk, and took a gulp.

That-a-boy. The beast sharpened its beak on a wing spike.

After a few minutes, Ruby opened her door. "Whatcha doing?"

"Give me a couple minutes. It's a surprise."

"I don't like surprises," Ruby said, puffing her hair. She pulled out her lipstick and used the side-view mirror to apply it.

Edward stared at the hammer in the trunk.

The Darkness fluttered its wings in anticipation of the kill.

"Come on back here. I want to show you something." Edward said, smooth as glass.

Ruby stepped between the larger rocks. "What?" she said as she came around the back.

The shadow flew from the opened door to Edward's shoulder, dug in, and waited for the rush as life seeped out of Ruby.

"This."

He lifted the hammer, slid it to the side of the trunk, pulled a small cooler forward, and opened it. A bottle of Dom Perignon sat in icy water. "I plan on making my relationship with Caitlyn exclusive. There's no one else. I load the ice every morning. You never know when you'll find a romantic place and a time that seems right."

"I feel like a fool," Ruby clucked. "I thought for sure it was an affair."

"That license has probably been there forever." He turned to Ruby. "I had a shot of scotch. Want one?"

"Absolutely," she said.

He emptied a plastic water bottle and poured her two shots.

The Darkness squawked from the roof of the car. *Click-clack.*

Edward glimpsed at Ruby's pearl-laden neck. Just the thought of taking her down made his breath deepen. *But not today. Definitely, not today. Too obvious.* Caitlyn would know he was the last person to see her.

Edward lifted the bottle of Johnnie Blue. "To life," he said.

Ruby lifted hers high. "*L'chaim.*"

They gulped down the scotch, got in the car, and rode back to Ruby's in silence.

CHAPTER 18

AFTER EDWARD DROPPED Ruby off and went through her house to ensure she was safe, The Darkness pushed him until he hit the road to look for a score. A few hours before dawn, just on the outskirts of Ogden, Utah, he picked up a girl who didn't know she was hitching her last ride. The murder was simple. He pulled off onto a side road and strangled the co-ed who "liked to hitchhike for fun." Edward and The Darkness had a good chuckle on that because she'd been right, it had been fun.

Although Edward's estate was his refuge, driving brought him comfort as well. Drawn to Las Vegas—his home away from home—he enjoyed gambling, shopping, fine dining, entertainment, and nightlife. Most of all, he liked the ease of disappearing into the crowd.

At noon the next day, Edward drove into Las Vegas and went to his condo for a nap. He awoke around three in the afternoon, had an early dinner, and headed to the casinos.

Sitting at a cocktail table across from Caesar's fifty-thousand-gallon saltwater aquarium, Edward watched as people passed him. There were women in flowing gowns; in halter tops and short shorts; jeans and t-shirts. Several walked on heels so high, they looked like they were tiptoeing. All of them easy prey.

Occasionally, he'd glance at the giant tank to appear normal, but his focus would drift back to the women. Like a jungle cat engrossed as zebra grazed, Edward saw himself as a lion. *The king—*

—Of spades. The Darkness cut in. *Let's hit the blackjack tables. I'm feeling lucky.*

I have to stop at Tiffany's first, Edward replied.

When did you become such a romantic? clucked the beast.

After almost four months of dating, it's time to seal the deal. Patrick Derry's daughter will be mine!

After stopping at Tiffany's and buying an exquisite necklace, he hit the casino and won $4500, enough to cover the gift.

CHAPTER 19

"WHEN'S EDWARD COMING back?" Ruby glanced at the clock and slid the brisket in her oven.

"He said he'll be back tomorrow night." Cate glanced at her cell phone. "He called me when he got there, but I haven't heard from him since."

"Why don't you call him then?" Ruby said, seeing the disappointment on Cate's face.

"I'm surprised you didn't say 'he must be having an affair.'"

Ruby shrugged, tightened the bandana around her curlers, and adjusted the curl taped in front of each ear.

Cate always wondered if Ruby noticed the rectangular red marks the tape left on her skin.

"Not my business." Even without her lashes, foundation, eyeshadow, blush, or eyeliner, Ruby kept those lips red. "Will's the keeper."

"I can't believe you invited him to dinner."

"That was days ago, and now you're blabbering about that?"

"I'm not interested in a cop. I don't like them."

"I trust him," Ruby replied. "Edward. He's just . . ." She gestured with her hands as she spoke, and her bracelets jingled. "A *gonif*."

"With the Yiddish. What the heck does that mean?"

"Shady. Clever. Tricky." Ruby finished grinding the chicken liver. "And he's all three."

"Why do you keep going on like this? I know you don't like him. A personality clash, that's all. You're both so . . . willful."

"I'll finish the chopped liver and get myself dolled up. Come back by four-thirty."

"Yes, ma'am." Cate saluted, did a fast turn, and marched out the door.

THAT NIGHT, AFTER a delicious dinner and entertaining conversation, Will offered to walk Cate next door to her home. With the Copycat still on the loose, women felt vulnerable—even going a short distance without an escort was inadvisable.

"That Ruby sure is a kick. Those red leather pants and tiger-striped getup she was wearing—whoa, dear mama—and those red shoes."

"She's like that. She puts her own spin on things."

Already at Cate's door, they looked at each other, but neither one of them said anything. The silence was uncomfortable enough for Cate to blurt, "Want to come in for coffee?" *Gosh, darn! Why did I feel like I had to fill in the silence? Now he's coming in. Why don't I think before I speak?*

"I sure enough could use a coffee infusion."

Will took a seat on the couch and glanced at the large-screen TV. "Ever seen *Total Recall?*"

"I'm more of a romance kind of—"

"Goodness gracious, you've gotta see it. I've been fixin' to see it again for the last two weeks."

Is he asking me to watch it now? What am I supposed to do? I'll say I'm tired. I'm tired and want to—

"But you're probably whooped after helping Ruby cook all day."

"No, not at all." *Jeepers. I've got to keep my freaking mouth shut.*

AFTER A FEW days in Vegas, Edward was on his way back. When he reached Washington, he drove into a wall of rain. The downpour fought him as he continued northwest. The closer he came to Seattle, the thicker the traffic became. Stuck in the stop-and-go that soon became a crawl, his travel time slowed, and he didn't pull into town until after ten that night.

Edward knew Caitlyn was not working tonight, and he looked forward to surprising her a day early. When he reached her house, it pleased him to see the living room lamp casting a glow. Often, if bored late at night, Edward would drive by Caitlyn's home. When the light was on, Caitlyn was awake. She had her routine. On rare occasions, he'd peek into her windows just for the hell of it.

Tonight was one of those nights. Not wanting to alarm Caitlyn if she'd nodded off while watching TV, he parked the car around the block and snuck through backyards until he reached her window. He glimpsed through the partially closed blinds. On the couch, having a laugh, sat Caitlyn and some asshole.

Fury ripped through Edward. He clamped his fists so tight that his fingernails left deep grooves imprinted on his palms. The Darkness pounced from the eaves and landed squarely on his back. Drilling its stinger into Edward's spine, the ferocious creature egged him on.

Kill that cheating bitch, The Darkness screeched.

Edward stood at the window, paralyzed. Although he wanted to tear down her door, snuff out that prick, and destroy Caitlyn, he knew he couldn't. *Not Patrick Derry's daughter. Not the best of all his trophies.* Smeared in her deceitfulness, his face burned. Caitlyn was his. Yet, she sat inside, laughing it up, while he suffocated outside. He thought about the necklace he'd bought her—rage blinded him.

He had to destroy someone. Now.

And then he realized a way to punish Caitlyn and take care of Ruby with one small action. Oh, yeah, he'd teach them both a thing or two. Show them that "the choices we make matter"—thank you, Dr. Phil. He stumbled from Caitlyn's window to Ruby's backyard. With eyes like embers, The Darkness scorched through Edward.

Click-clack. Click-clack—the noise magnified in the night.

I've got this, Edward muttered. *So shut the fuck up.*

Louder and louder, the repetitive *click-clacking* spurred him on. Without thought, he jiggled the back-window screen until it came off, jimmied the window open, and climbed in.

RUBY OPENED HER eyes. What had brought her out of her dream? She wasn't sure, but she was awake. She lay in bed, alert but not moving. The whirl of the ceiling fan hummed a dark melody. A couple of blades, slightly off-balance, caused the fan to thump like a lazy heart. *Tha-dump. Tha-dump* with each slow revolution. *Tha-dump.*

The room was in complete darkness, yet Ruby felt a presence. In the distance, she heard a car door bang and a dog bark. She thought of jumping out of bed, opening the bedroom window, and screaming for help. But deep in her psyche, she already knew it was too late.

She inched her arm to the headboard and reached for the baseball bat she kept "just in case." Blindly, she moved her hand between the bed and the night table. Fear clogged her throat. Her stomach knotted. *Where was the bat?*

She reached in the space a second time, circling her hand faster and faster. *Nothing.*

Her pulse thudded in her ear. Could she drop to the floor and slip under the bed without being heard? The bathroom nightlight was off. Had she left it off? She never did. Why was there no glow?

The room was black.

"Ruby?" The voice was close.

Not daring to move, Ruby lay there, silent.

"Do you know what our Caitlyn is doing tonight?"

"Edward? Is that you?" Ruby sat up in bed. "I'm turning on the light."

"Don't you fucking touch the light, bitch." The bat touched her leg. "Who the fuck is Caitlyn with tonight?"

"It's not what you think . . . he's a cop. He's been snooping around, asking Cate personal questions and—"

"I know *exactly* what's going on."

Edward clicked the light on and stood over Ruby, baseball bat in hand.

"Edward, please, let me explain—"

He lifted the bat, and with one powerful swing, he slammed Ruby's head so hard he cracked her skull to reveal the grayish-pink matter of her brain.

CHAPTER 20

IT WAS CATE who called Will the next afternoon.

"Ruby's car's in the driveway, but she's not answering her door nor her phone. Something's wrong. I can feel it. I've got a spare key, but I'm afraid to go in."

Will tried to calm Cate and promised he was on his way. Less than a half-hour later, Will entered Ruby's bedroom. As if she'd been dragged, Ruby lay in a crumpled pile in the corner of her bed. Her head and body had been severely beaten. Next to her was a bloody baseball bat. The killer had been so ferocious, he'd obliterated Ruby's face during the beating. Blood splatters reached as far as her bedroom door.

"I don't understand," Cate cried. "I was right next door. Ruby locks her doors. Why would someone . . .?"

With the crime scene to contend with, Will couldn't console Cate, so she called Edward hoping he'd made it home from Vegas.

"Someone killed Ruby. They took a baseball bat and destroyed her."

"Dear God," Edward said, lounging in the screening room of his estate. "I'll get there as soon as I can. I'm still six hours from Seattle."

Once fellow officers arrived on the scene, Will took time to sit with Cate, who was a wreck. She had nowhere to turn with Ruby gone and Edward on the road. Will offered to bring her lunch, but she just needed the company.

CHAPTER 21

AFTER EDWARD WORKED through his rage—after all, he was not an animal, he always cooled off—he came to terms with what he had seen through the window the night before. Ruby had said the jerk was a cop. *What the fuck was a cop doing laughing it up with Caitlyn?*

Did Edward feel bad he had taken his anger out on Ruby? Of course not. She had been too nosy. Too stubborn. In the way. "When you choose the behavior, you choose the consequences," says Dr. Phil. *And he's right.*

Edward pulled into Caitlyn's driveway. The activity next door had subsided, and all that was left was yellow crime scene tape wrapped around Ruby's property. When he knocked on Caitlyn's door, a bald guy opened it.

Curled up in the couch's corner, Caitlyn looked up at Edward, her eyes swollen from crying. Edward rushed to her, and she burst into tears.

"Caitlyn, honey." Edward pushed past the fucker who'd answered the door. The same asshole he'd seen on Caitlyn's couch the night before.

"Oh, Edward," was all she could manage.

Edward wrapped her in his arms and turned to the Vin Diesel look-alike. "And you are?"

"Detective Will Cambrey." Will extended his hand. "I'm investigating the Copycat killings."

"Edward Olson." Edward shook Will's hand, his grip tighter than it needed to be. "Caitlyn's *boyfriend*." His instinct was to kill the jerk right there, but the last thing he needed was to murder a cop. *When one of their own goes down, they're like pit bulls.*

An awkward silence swept the room.

"He's following up on Ruby's murder, too. He thinks they might be connected," Caitlyn muttered.

Edward noticed Will shoot Caitlyn a hard glare.

"Whoops." She pretended to zip her mouth shut.

"What makes you think they're connected?" Edward tried to make small talk while he seethed with jealousy.

"My gut." Will sat back down. "Caitlyn mentioned you knew Ruby."

"Met her a couple of times. She came over for dinner with Caitlyn not too long ago. I gave her a ride home," Edward said. "A nice woman. I liked her."

"You were in Vegas yesterday?" Will asked.

"I left for home about ten yesterday morning."

"That's a long drive to do overnight."

"Takes me about eighteen hours if I drive straight through. I'm used to it," Edward said, the words like butter in his mouth. "Just got back into town. I came straight here." He turned to Caitlyn. "You okay?"

Caitlyn nodded.

"Where d'you stay in Vegas?"

"I have a condo there. What's with the questions?"

"Just crossing all my T's."

"Well, unless you are going to arrest me for something, I'm done answering them." Edward took a slow breath. *Easy now. Easy.* "So, what happened to Ruby?"

"She was murdered last night," Will said.

"Yeah, I know that. *What* happened?"

"Someone beat her," Caitlyn sobbed.

"Any leads?" Edward turned to Will.

"Not yet."

As Edward's gaze met Will's, he thought about what it would take to bring the prick down. Will's eyes looked like he was thinking the same thing.

Will broke his glare first, a victory as far as Edward was concerned.

"You okay now, Cate?" Will said.

Caitlyn nodded.

Will grabbed his jacket.

Caitlyn pulled herself up from the couch and met Will at the door. "Thanks for everything." She hugged him.

"See y'all around."

Caitlyn closed the door.

Edward gave Caitlyn time to return to the sofa then struck.

"Does *everyone* get personal condolences when a neighbor is killed?" Edward honed the edge in his voice.

"Will's a friend," Cate replied.

"Since when? You've never mentioned him." The thought of Will hanging around bothered Edward. First, the prick's a cop. And second, the bastard has more on his mind than friendship. And last, he detested people messing with his property.

"He's a new friend. I met him at the hospital while he was investigating the disappearance of Sarah Bloom. I didn't know who else to call when Ruby didn't answer the door."

"Yeah?" Edward attempted to steady his voice.

"Ruby's dead, and you're having a jealousy fit? *Really?*" She broke into tears.

Edward took a second to regroup. *Oh right, I need to act sad.*

"I'm sorry. I'm just not myself. Ruby's death has stunned me too." Edward tried to sound choked up. "I feel so helpless." He hesitated then sighed.

There, that should do it.

"I'm afraid to stay here tonight. Pipsqueak sleeps like a bear in hibernation—he's no help," Cate said.

"I could stay with you," Edward replied. "Or you could come to my place."

"Do you think it could have been the Copycat? Could he have been watching me and gone to the wrong house? I mean, he usually goes for younger—"

"You've been watching too much news. Come on, you know you'll be safe at my house."

CHAPTER 22

WILL LEANED BACK in his chair and closed his eyes. *Something about the Ruby Valin case didn't make sense. What was it? Why would the Copycat want to get rid of an eightyish-year-old woman, and why?*

Will gathered the facts and scribbled on his notepad. Sure, he might-could use his iPad, but it was darn near separating him from his connection to the cases. Lord willin' and the creek don't rise, this boy's goin' to make a mistake.

> The lace ribbon meant the Copycat.
>
> Miss Ruby was elderly, why would the Copycat go and choose her?
>
> I reckon her death was personal—so he knew her.
>
> What in tarnation triggered rage enough to obliterate Miss Ruby asleep in bed?
>
> Who were the people around her?

One of those people would be Caitlyn Derry, daughter of an infamous serial killer. Did she get a murderous streak from her daddy? But Will had been with Cate near the time of the crime, had fallen asleep on her couch. What would have whipped Cate into that kind of rage? Will shook his head. That dog won't hunt.

Then there was this boy, Edward. Will had a bad feeling about him from the start. But he was out of town . . . wasn't he?

CHAPTER 23

LACE RIBBON TIES SKELETAL REMAINS TO COPYCAT. Edward scanned the front page of the paper. He took pride in his work and was pleased about this latest discovery. He was a celebrity now, and the public recognized his style. With his notoriety, he felt he should branch out. Maybe he'd write a letter to the newspaper? The Zodiac Killer had used a code—impressive. He could taunt the police, but that was so cliché. What if he disguised his voice and called a radio station? Say hello to the women of Seattle?

"Honey?" Caitlyn came from the kitchen into the living room of her new condo in Redmond. "Did you even hear what I said?"

"Huh?" Edward snapped out of his thoughts.

"I said I appreciate your help with the move."

"I hired a truck and some guys. Big deal. You feeling safe is what matters."

"I feel much better," she said sweetly. "I love this place—but gosh . . . so many boxes to unpack."

It had been a month since Ruby's funeral. They'd held the closed casket ceremony on a drizzly morning. Simple. Elegant. Ruby had no family and not much of an estate, so Edward covered the cost. It was the least he could do.

Edward was in good spirits, but Caitlyn's disposition fluctuated. Apparently, she was torn between the joy she felt with him and the grief from Ruby's murder. Either way, her moods were difficult to predict.

"Looking forward to work today?"

"You know I'm not. The temporary supervisor has been on me. I'm the lowest on the totem pole—when things go wrong, the team looks to the newbie first. That's the way it in hospitals. I despise the politics."

"Why didn't you take time off to grieve like they suggested? We could leave tomorrow. Get away."

"I don't want them to think I'm weak."

"Is it weak to be sad?" It was meant to be a rhetorical question, but he *was* curious.

Caitlyn sighed. "I guess you're right. I can't wait to see your apartment."

"Honey, it's a cubby hole with a bed," Edward lied. "I'd rather make our stay special. We'll get the Vista suite at the Mandalay Bay—it's got a 180-degree view of the strip."

They were in Las Vegas for dinner the next evening. Room service brought a feast, and they drank a bottle of wine between them. Caitlyn, with her low tolerance for alcohol, was tipsy after her first glass.

"Don't get drunk," Edward warned with a laugh. "I've got a surprise for you."

"A surprise?" Caitlyn's words slurred just enough to add cuteness to her already adorable self.

"But first, my famous Vegas joke. Why did the sesame seed not want to leave the casino?"

"Because . . ."

"Because it was on a roll."

Caitlyn giggled.

"Ready for that surprise?"

Caitlyn nodded; her eyes filled with excitement.

"Come with me" He took her hand and led her to the bedroom mirror. "Look at how stunning you are," he murmured. "You're the only woman I want."

"Oh, Edward," Caitlyn cooed.

"I got you this as a token of our exclusivity. I mean, should you say yes."

Caitlyn blushed as Edward handed her the Tiffany Blue Box. She slowly pulled the white ribbon.

Ah, if only the ribbon had been lace, The Darkness said. *It would have been such a nice touch.*

Stop. Edward glared at the creature who perched on a chair.

Caitlyn opened the lid to reveal a gorgeous diamond necklace.

"I can't believe how beautiful—"

"As beautiful as you." Edward took the necklace from the box, stood behind Caitlyn, and put it around her neck.

"Oh, my gosh." The magnificent stones sparkled.

"Will you be my girl?" Edward wrapped his arms around Caitlyn.

"Yes. Yes," Caitlyn muttered, seemingly dazzled by the gift.

Edward caressed her cheek. "Then, we're exclusive?"

Caitlyn gave Edward a gentle kiss.

"Oh, baby," Edward whispered. "You don't know how long I've waited for this moment."

With one hand on the small of her back, Edward brought Caitlyn even closer. Although ambivalent about sex—sex with a live woman seemed so disrespectful—Edward knew that he should make a move. He lifted Caitlyn and carried her to the king-size bed.

"I want you," Edward said.

"I want you, too," Caitlyn whispered. "Can I tell you something first?"

Edward climbed into bed next to her and propped himself up, resting on his elbow. "Sure. You know you can talk to me about anything."

"There's something I haven't told you." Caitlyn sat up. "You might change your mind about me."

"What is it?"

Caitlyn buried her face in her hands. "Do you know who Patrick Derry was?"

"The serial killer?" Edward asked. *Where the hell was she going with this?*

Caitlyn nodded. "He was my father."

"Whew, that's tough."

"I worry that . . . I mean if I ever have a child . . . it will inherit his genes."

Edward took her hands in his. "Sweetie, he's *your* father, and you're okay."

"You're not worried?"

"About you? Or the child?" Edward tried to lift the mood and smiled.

"Both." With that, Caitlyn fell into tears.

Edward felt himself cringe. Caitlyn's constant crying since Ruby's death had worn on him. He grabbed his bottle of scotch from his suitcase and downed a gulp. Then another. And another.

"Here." He poured some whiskey into a glass, dropped a dull green caplet into the drink, and handed it to her. "This will take the edge off."

Caitlyn shook her head. "I'm not on edge."

Edward grabbed her arm. "Drink it."

"Ouch, Edward." Caitlyn tried to pull her arm from his grasp. "You're hurting me."

"Drink it. You'll feel better."

Caitlyn took the glass, had a sip, and attempted to hand it back to Edward.

"Again. Now," he insisted.

Caitlyn drank another shot.

"Finish it."

Across the room, the flap, flap, flap of the beast's wings distracted Edward. The whishing sound got louder until it morphed into the *click-clack* of the beak.

Stay there," Without thinking, Edward shouted out loud to The Darkness. "I've got this covered."

"Got what covered . . ." Caitlyn tried to climb off the bed but collapsed back to the mattress.

"Don't move," Edward mumbled.

"But—"

"Be quiet. No talking."

"But I—" Caitlyn said moments before she passed out.

"Caitlyn?" Edward shook her. "Caitlyn, wake up."

Nothing.

Satisfied that she was out, he pulled Caitlyn to the middle of the bed, crawled on top of her, and pushed himself into her seemingly lifeless body.

After, Edward lay on his back and wished he could smoke a joint. He knew he shouldn't have drugged her. But it made sense. She would never have volunteered to play dead. I mean, even *he* knew how creepy his request would sound.

CATE AWOKE IN the suite, her head throbbing. The clock glowed two-thirty. She stumbled into the bathroom and vomited. The bathroom spun, and she vomited again. She lay on the tiled bathroom floor in her disheveled cocktail dress, for how long, she wasn't sure.

After clicking on the light, Cate pulled herself up and stumbled to the mirror. Her mascara had smeared into dark circles under her eyes. Fingertip-shaped bruises marked both arms. Her body ached.

"Edward?" Cate called into the darkened bedroom. "I don't feel so good."

Cate rinsed her face with cold water.

"Edward?"

Cate worked her way back to the bed and fell in. She reached for Edward, but his side of the bed was empty. Too sick from nausea, Cate returned to sleep before she had time to consider where Edward might be.

"GAMBLING," EDWARD SAID over breakfast in bed. "I was gone for an hour or so."

"I feel sick," Cate complained.

"Drink your juice; it'll help."

"You know," Cate whispered, "I have bruises. And I hurt."

"It was the scotch." Edward tapped his foot under the table. "We shouldn't have had so much to drink. I'm sorry."

Cate shrugged. "No, need." She turned her head away as the flush of embarrassment heated her face. *Dare she tell him?* She glanced at Edward and had to admit, she felt protected by his strength. And loved. "To be honest, I like it."

"You like what?" Edward gently lifted her chin and turned her face toward him.

"The bruises. The aching. I know we must have had sex, and I'm embarrassed to say, I barely remember it. Weird, right?"

"Every time you reveal something about yourself, I love you more." Edward crossed his arms and leaned back against the headboard. He looked content. "Want to get married while we're here?"

"Not funny," Cate said, her voice sinking.

"I'm not kidding." Edward leaned closer to Cate. "We're two peas in a pod."

"We are?"

"I've got an idea. Stay right here."

Edward was out of the restaurant before Cate could answer. In less than five minutes, he was back with a bouquet of roses.

"To the first day of our exclusivity." He handed her the velvet-soft purple roses.

"They're beautiful."

"Marry me tonight?"

Cate smiled but said nothing. Her future was too uncertain to make any long-term commitments. Even her job had her concerned. There had been no more suspicious deaths at the hospital since Sarah went missing. Everyone was certain that "the Angel of Death" *was* Sarah. Maybe all would be okay now? Cate doubted it would. Her life was never that simple.

CHAPTER 24

ON THE WAY back from Las Vegas, Edward watched the road while Caitlyn slept. As he passed through different parts of the route, he often reminisced about women he'd picked up along the highway. Driving allowed him to savor each detail.

But not today.

Today, Edward's one thought orbited within his mind. Caitlyn didn't seem to mind his rough side, his edginess, his propensity for violence. He remembered how she'd seen him fuck up the guy who accosted her in the park—her eyes had sparkled, and she'd grabbed his hand.

She's seen this side of me and still likes me. Would it be possible to show her more? It was lonely not having anyone to share his innermost thoughts—to know he was a pariah in society. There was no one to relax with. No one to help him on rough days. He imagined what it would be like to be honest with someone . . . and they not run in horror. Or go to the police. Or have him killed.

Maybe, with Caitlyn's help, he could escape The Darkness' hold over him. Perhaps one day, he could reclaim his soul.

Caitlyn opened her eyes and smiled. "Where are we?"

"We're in Oregon."

"Are you still mad?" Cate stretched and sat up straight in the seat.

"I'm not mad, Caitlyn. I'm disappointed."

"It was just too fast—I can't get married like that."

"Because of that cop?"

"Will's just a friend."

"I understand people's motives, and that guy's hot for you. I don't want you to see him anymore."

Caitlyn laughed. "Really? Since when are you the boss of me?" She dropped the sun visor, checked her reflection in the mirror, and tied her hair into a makeshift knot.

"Since we became exclusive."

"Well, I'm not interested in pursuing anything with the guy. I can let that friendship go."

"That's my girl." Edward patted Caitlyn's thigh.

"But you're not the boss of me, you know that, right?" Caitlyn looked directly at Edward.

"Okay. Sure."

CHAPTER 25

ALTHOUGH WILL MET with Cate for lunch once a week, the conflict about his feeling for Cate dragged with him as if his mind was in a cement block. Each thought about her, each moment they spent together contradicted the code of conduct. Having a relationship with someone he met while performing his duties was cause for dismissal. This was not like Will. He had always been aboveboard and ethical. Until Cate.

Her innocent demeanor and her shyness attracted him. *Bless her heart.* Even though he knew Cate and Edward were hog wild for each other, he figured soon enough she'd see Edward's dirty laundry. Will had only met Edward a few times but knew that the guy was up to no-good.

Why?

Edward was like sandpaper on silk with his jealousy and controlling nature. Sure, Will saw the draw—Edward's good looks, his money, and his charisma, but he knew that something was off. He just couldn't figure out what.

Will's mind shot right back to his conflict. His ex-partner had dated a witness to a crime and realized too late that her attention bordered on psychotic. When he tried to break it off, she made a single call to the chief, and Will's partner was fired. That's how Will ended up with the new detective, LaKeisha Taylor, by his side.

LaKeisha was nice enough and smart as Einstein. Her hair was as red as an overripe, plump tomato. Full and curly. Often mistaken for Chaka Kha, she'd give autographs using her real name when asked to sign something. She dressed in high fashion no matter where she went but only wore flats on the job.

"What's up, Will. You seem a million miles away," LaKeisha said.

Will scanned Spud and then brought his focus back to LaKeisha. "Naw, just chewing on the Copycat case."

"Are you going to finish that piece of fish?"

"You eat like Virginia opossum."

"How's that?"

"They ain't picky, and they eat other animals' leftovers."

"Are you eating it or not?"
"You go right ahead and eat it. Finish these here chips too."

CHAPTER 26

CATE CHOSE NOT to mention her continuing friendship with Will. Edward traveled out of town on business at least once every couple weeks. Since Ruby's murder, being home alone at night was still a challenge for Cate. When Edward traveled, Will often kept her company. He'd do card tricks with his lucky deck, chat for hours, share dinner, and watch movies until Cate went to bed. Occasionally, he'd fall asleep on the couch, wake up around two, and drive home.

Cate took advantage of her friendship with Will and tried to extract information on Ruby's murder and the Copycat. Her intuition told her that the Copycat and Ruby's murderer were the same. She had that kind of mind. Must have inherited it from her father.

But Will was discrete—only occasionally would he mention what was going on in the investigation. "We reckon he's moved on, in prison, or just plain stopped," he had told her the last time they met for lunch.

He's moved on. Thank God.

Now that she was back from Las Vegas, things settled back to normal. She loved her new condo and felt safer in a gated community. At work, rumors lingered that Sarah Bloom was responsible for the hospital deaths, which gratified Cate. She was glad the pack of gossipy nurses had something better to discuss than her. After all, the newbie was considered worthless.

The Pyxis dispense system's problems continued, keeping the technician busy. Thankful that they didn't have to hassle with the machine while it was in repair, Cate and the other nurses had better access to medications.

Overwhelmed with paperwork, the new supervisor on five-east spent less time micro-managing the nurses. The pressure on the floor nurses lessened. Cate went to and from work in good spirits.

All was well.

That is until a twenty-three-year-old athlete died in critical care. Just upgraded from critical to serious, Craig Tersen showed signs of improvement. His mother had informed the family of this happy turn of events when Dr. Remmington, the on-call surgeon, approached her.

Even Cate, in the elevator rising between floors four and five, heard the howl. There's a difference, Cate knew, between a scream of terror and one of absolute grief. The cry from five-east sounded like unbearable anguish. She knew she'd be needed and felt grateful to be involved.

The elevator doors opened. Around the corner and down the hall, Mrs. Tersen stood hysterical. Remmington and two floor nurses surrounded her. Cate hurried to Craig's mother, who she'd often chatted with when she visited her unconscious son. Cate had encouraged Mrs. Tersen to talk to Craig, read to him, and play his favorite music.

Mrs. Tersen saw Cate and rushed to her open arms. "But he was improving," she sobbed.

Cate's glance shifted to Dr. Remmington, who shook his head. Tersen had passed. Cate knew that her greatest asset was her ability to soothe the bereaved. She showcased this on her resume and was called upon in these situations.

Cate walked Mrs. Tersen to the hospital chapel and sat with her in the otherwise vacant pews. Speaking in a calm voice, Cate consoled her. Cate understood loss. From the moment they had taken her father away, an emptiness had swept through her that was never filled.

The day they came for Patrick Derry, gloominess draped Cate's world like a mist in a graveyard. Barren trees clawed at the sky, and winter's rain pounded the ground. Cate had answered the door. She had pointed to the gray shed when they asked about her father. If she had known he was in trouble, she would have told them her daddy wasn't home.

As they took Derry away—his head hung low, his hands locked behind his back—the KOMO news team cameras rolled, and a crowd had formed. That was the last time she saw him. The last time she was permitted to mention his name. Before too long, she and her mother moved to Tacoma to escape the public eye.

The emptiness felt like a desert. Barren and dry. Her mother's blame sat on Cate's shoulders like a boulder. "It was your carelessness that made him turn bad. If you had watched your sister better . . ." The words haunted Cate like a lonely ghost.

Cate handed Mrs. Tersen a tissue and took one to wipe away her own tears. It was in moments like this, as heartbreaking as they were, that Cate felt her self-worth climb. Helping others fed Cate's soul.

This was why she chose healthcare.

This was why she was such a darn fine nurse.

CHAPTER 27

CAITLYN ARRIVED HOME to find flowers on her stoop. This time it was a gorgeous mix of purple hydrangea, lavender roses, hot pink spray roses, and white freesia beautifully arranged and delivered in a divine Couture vase.

You love purple. I love you. Edward.

Every Friday since Las Vegas, Edward sent Caitlyn a bouquet.

"To remind you that I don't take you for granted," Edward said that evening.

"It's wonderful to come home to flowers on my porch. Especially today."

"Why today?" Edward took her hand.

"We lost a young man," Caitlyn murmured. "He had turned the corner and was ready to move out of critical, then he succumbed."

"Oh, sweetie, I'm so sorry." Edward wrapped Caitlyn in his arms. "I know how hard this stuff hits you."

Caitlyn shrugged. "It's starting to become the norm. Thank goodness I was there to soothe the mother."

"Do they think his death was intentional? Is that shit starting up again?" Edward pulled away and took Caitlyn's hand.

"Nothing's been said. Everyone's still reeling. But no, I don't think so." Caitlyn smiled. "I've been there for those families that have lost loved ones. Helping them soothes me."

"You're a good person, Caitlyn."

"Not really."

"Compare yourself with those other nurses on the floor. Only Scott has your kind of compassion and caring."

"I guess." Caitlyn pulled out a tube of lipstick and applied the "Mango Breeze" hue to her lips.

"Ah, daring. Since when do you wear a shade that isn't light pink?"

"Since today," Caitlyn replied. "I bought this color when I stopped at CVS."

"What did the duck say when she bought lipstick?" Edward smiled.

"I don't know. What?"

"Just put it on my bill."

"Gosh!" Caitlyn shook her head.

"A bit of Ruby has rubbed off on you," Edward said then smiled. "I miss her quirkiness. She was a sweetheart."

"That Copycat Killer has a black hole instead of a soul." Caitlyn spat out the words.

"You think?" Edward almost whispered. "No soul at all?"

Caitlyn shrugged.

"Your father had a soul, right? He was a good man driven by his demons. He couldn't help himself."

"You think Daddy was a good man even though he murdered those women?"

"He loved *you*, didn't he?"

"So evil can be good too?"

"What do you think? You loved him even though—"

"Yes. I still do."

"What if you had known the truth all along? Would you have still loved him?"

"Of course, I would have." Caitlyn squeezed Edward's hand. "Love is unconditional."

Edward scooped Caitlyn into his arms and carried her down the hall to her bedroom. After laying her on the bed, he sat down next to her, lifted her hair from across her eyes, and kissed her along her forehead, down her face, to her neck.

"Oh, Edward." Caitlyn sighed.

"I wish I could be more like you." Edward's voice flowed like a lazy stream. "You feel so deeply and aren't afraid to share who you are, no matter what others think." And he *sort of* meant it. Although he didn't understand the concepts and feelings associated with emotions, it was curious to him that other people seemed to find something pleasing when they talked about private things, when they touched, and when they were in love.

Edward lay down and took her in his arms. He knew how to touch softly, talk sweetly, and seem like he was opening up, but it was just a series of lies— heavy links connected like snow chains to disguise the winter storm in his heart.

"You are such a beauty, my love," Edward murmured as he unbuttoned her top, slowly. Sensuously.

With all the tenderness he could muster, Edward made love to her until she fell into a passionate swirl of moaning and soft tears.

THAT LATE AFTERNOON, Edward sat in his sunroom, glad to be home. Alone. He kicked back a shot of Johnnie Blue and let the heat burn through him. Light drizzling misted the glass walls, and he felt cushioned in a cloud. The silence cocooned him.

Love is unconditional.

The words hung in his mind like Christmas lights.

If she could love her father who'd killed women for sport, perhaps she could love me too.

Caitlyn had shared dark truths with Edward—about her childhood, her feelings, and being Patrick Derry's daughter. He was impressed she'd had the guts. She had shared with him something that he knew must be special, although he could neither feel it nor know how to react.

You looked into her soul, The Darkness muttered.

Her soul? Edward repeated. *What the hell am I supposed to do with that?* He was a boardwalk amid carnival rides.

One thing Edward knew for sure; The Darkness had stolen his soul. Even at age eight, his foster parents told him he had no soul when they caught him dissecting a live rabbit. How could he have explained to them it wasn't him— it was this "monster" that had grabbed on and wouldn't let go?

What should you do with it? The shadow clucked. *Show her the lost soul you are.*

What?

She'd like that. You should keep your trophy happy, what with that slimy cop hanging around like a rat in an alleyway.

I don't have a soul. You fucking stole it, Edward said, his voice guttural.

Here we go. The Darkness climbed up Edward's spine to his shoulder. *You want to have that conversation?* He pecked Edward hard on the cheek.

Goddammit. Edward pushed the entity off his shoulder. *My soul's been hijacked, and you know it.*

Perhaps if you showed your Caitlyn the real you, you'd get your soul back. Right, boss?

Whatever, Edward said, not wanting to engage in an argument. Maybe, if he could be open like Caitlyn had been, and she accepted him, it would give him access to his soul. What would it be like to not carry the shadow of death wherever he went? What would it feel like to love and be loved?

Knowing Caitlyn had offered him a glimpse of her precious soul should mean something. Right?

But, seriously, what was he supposed to do with it?

CHAPTER 28

CATE COULD FEEL how much her patients' families relied on her. She was the only nurse that allowed compassion to seep into her time on the floor. Without her, most families would have no one to talk to, to lean on, to understand their needs when their loved one's life was balanced on the precipice of death.

Mostly hardnosed nurses, who had long ago learned to separate their hearts from their jobs, worked with the critical care patients. Cate realized the challenge and stress created from being empathetic day after day—many days, she even had to fake it. But most nurses had shut down their emotions. Not Cate.

"If I ever become like that," Cate had said to Edward, "just shoot me. There's no sense in being a nurse."

Consequently, Cate often came home from work in tears.

"I hate to see you so upset," Edward said when she walked in the door after a night shift.

Although sometimes he'd talk about his feelings, Cate often noticed he didn't seem connected to his words. Cate figured he had PTSD from the death of his parents when he was a child.

"Marry me, Caitlyn. You can quit work and stay home taking care of our baby."

"I know my worries are a sort of obsessive, but the possibility of raising a child with my dad's problems . . ."

"If you want a baby, I'll help you take care of the little critter, but it's not important to me to have one."

"You say that now," Cate replied. "People change their minds after they get married. I've read all about it in magazines."

TO AVOID THE stress of keeping his true self from Caitlyn and putting up with her ever-winding jack-in-the-box emotions, Edward spent a lot of his free time fighting The Darkness' desire to "shut her up for good." A shot of scotch in the morning took the edge off, a couple more around lunch, then during and after dinner.

As if he trekked uphill with a boulder on his back, the pressure not to succumb to the creature's complaining weighed on him. When he added drugs to the mix, the nagging morphed to background chatter. That morning, he'd had a serendipitous encounter with his dealer in Home Depot. After a brief discussion, Edward resurrected his erratic love affair with cocaine.

He bought a half ounce and spent the next few days snorting it. Sure, he hung out with Caitlyn, but he didn't mention his cocaine binge. He stayed up late and got up early. Moody, irritable, and easily provoked, he picked at her the entire two days she was at his home.

"Must you cry?" Edward said while they watched *Titanic* at his house that evening.

"It's a sad movie." Caitlyn wiped her tears.

"You can't go five minutes without sobbing," Edward growled. "And the picking at your nails could drive a person nuts. Can't you sit still?"

"Me? *I'm* not still? You're the one racing around the house like an untied balloon. What's gotten into you?"

"It's always me, right, Caitlyn? I'm the one that causes all the problems."

"Are you mad at me?"

"Sometimes, you get on my nerves." Edward's barbed words hit their mark. "Can't I have just a few days of peace?"

"Ouch," Caitlyn said. "Why didn't you say so?"

"I just did." Edward got up, flicked off the TV, stomped into his office, and slammed the door behind him.

"Well, fudge to you," Cate shouted. She grabbed her coat and headed out the door.

CHAPTER 29

"I GOT ON his nerves yesterday." Cate wrapped a turkey sandwich and bagged chips. With Ruby gone, it was nice to have a friend she could talk to.

"How's that?" Will asked.

"I cried during *Titanic*." Cate finished packing her dinner and searched for her keys. She had to be at work in forty-five minutes.

"Jesus. That's it?" Will shook his head.

"Plus, I picked the clear polish off my nails."

"I don't like that guy."

"Oh, Will. You barely know him. He's just moody lately." Cate handed Will his jacket and grabbed hers. "His law practice is very stressful."

Will picked up Pipsqueak, who gave him a big lick across the mouth. "Whoa, killer." He put Pipsqueak back on the floor.

"Pipsy loves the police." Cate picked Pipsqueak up. "Ruby didn't like Edward either—until she got to know him."

"I've got a nose for trouble, and he's trouble."

Cate laughed. "He's jealous of you; that's all."

"Little ole me?" Will said.

"Edward's got a nose for trouble too." Cate winked at Will.

"You want to do a movie night tomorrow here at your place?"

"Sure, Edward left this morning and won't be back for a couple of days."

"We gotta date. Is seven okay?"

Cate grabbed her dinner and then kissed Will on the cheek. "Seven is good. Let's go, Trouble." She opened the front door. "See you tomorrow."

WILL SHOWED UP the next night with pepperoni pizza. They did a crossword puzzle together, some card tricks, and then settled in for the movie. Will wore his sweats, and Cate got comfortable in her pajamas. Covered with small teddy bears, her PJs were just as sweet as her scrubs.

"Ta-da." Will pulled *War of the Worlds* from his coat and flashed it in front of Cate.

"I thought it was my turn to pick," Cate pouted. She held out *Home Again.* "I love Reese Witherspoon."

"Nope," Will said happily. "My night. Last time we watched *Sleepless in Seattle.*" He put his finger in his mouth and pretended to gag.

"Okay," Cate moaned. "Tom Cruise, it is."

Will slipped the DVD into the player and sat next to Cate on the couch.

THE BANGING WOKE Will first.

"What the—?" Will mumbled, still half asleep.

"Huh?" Cate muttered.

This time the pounding shook the door.

Cate jumped up from the couch and peered through the peephole. "Oh, God. It's Edward." She creaked the door open. "Honey." She forced a fake smile.

Edward pushed into the living room and glared at Will.

"Will's here." Cate tried to sound nonchalant. "I can explain." She went to hug him, but he pushed her aside.

"Hey, buddy," Will warned, standing up. "Watch how you treat the lady."

Ignoring Will, Edward turned back to Cate. "You fucking whore."

"I got scared. He came to watch a movie." Caitlyn's words smashed together like train cars in a crash.

"I got scared. He came to watch a movie." Edward mimicked Caitlyn's voice, then yelled, "In your pajamas!" He turned to Will. "Well, Officer, looks like y'all ain't needed here." He sneered.

Will looked like a bull ready to charge. "I'm not leaving until Cate asks me to leave."

"It's okay, Will." Caitlyn forced the words from her constricted throat. "Edward and I need to talk."

She glanced at Edward, who seemed ready to snap Will in half.

Will looked directly at Cate. "You call if you need me. And you." He turned his attention to Edward. "Watch yourself, or I'll find a good reason to put your ass in jail. You hear me?"

Edward's eyes seemed to follow Will's every move.

Will stared right back as he passed Edward.

"You sure, darlin'?" Will seemed hesitant—as if he knew things would go bad.

Cate nodded.

Will shot Edward a fierce glance, gave a wary nod to Cate, and walked out.

Edward gave the still opened door a shove to be sure it slammed and turned on Cate. "Fuck you."

"I didn't tell you that Will and I are still friendly 'cause I thought you'd misunderstand. And you have—"

"Oh, I understand just fine, and fuck you." Edward left, re-slamming the door behind him.

PARKED DOWN THE road from Cate's condo, Will had a good view of her living room window. He had stayed *just in case there was trouble.* But minutes after Will got in his car, Edward stormed out the door, jumped into his vehicle, and screeched down the street.

"You okay, darlin'?" Will had his phone on speaker as he started the car.

"He's so mad." Cate's voice trembled.

"You lock your doors and get some sleep. I've got something I have to do."

"You won't hurt him, right?"

"Nah, he's bigger than me." Will chuckled, said goodbye, and hung up.

Edward swerved.

Keeping a reasonable distance, Will followed Edward as he twisted and turned through different neighborhoods.

Where the crap is that lizard going?

Edward drove down a street, then sped up, rounded another corner, and did it again. This went on a good twenty minutes until Edward turned onto Aurora Avenue.

"Well, goddamn," Will muttered.

Edward pulled to the curb, and a woman wearing a mini skirt, halter-top, and large hoop earrings leaned into the passenger window. Minutes later, she climbed into the Altima, and Edward drove off.

Will thought of Cate, home alone and was torn. Should he follow Edward or check on Cate? He already knew what Edward's next move would be. Sex with the girl. *That no-good varmint is a cheat and a liar.* Will made a quick U-turn and headed back to Cate's.

"YOU SHOULDN'T BE here," Cate told Will as she opened the door. "He could come back any minute." She glanced up and down the street.

"Not for a while." Will couldn't help but notice her swollen eyes. "Did he touch you?" His tone was sharp.

"No." Tears trickled down her face. "I think it's over."

"He's not the right guy for you, Cate," Will said.

"You don't understand. There's magic between us."

"More like voodoo. He's a self-centered, jealous, rich boy who wants his way."

"We're kindred spirits," Cate said, heading for the kitchen. "And, he's taught me a lot about the world."

She came back with a bottle of Edward's Johnnie Blue. "This is my fault." Cate motioned to the bottle, and Will nodded.

"But you told him you weren't going to let him control you." Will had a shot.

Cate did the same, almost choking on the burn.

"You okay?"

"I'm not much of a drinker."

"I see that." Will smiled.

They each had another shot.

"He was the angriest I've ever seen him." Cate shook her head. "He wouldn't let me explain."

"Maybe he'll feel different in the morning. Give it time. It's tough to see you so crushed." He put his arm around her and pulled her in close. "Aw, sugar."

Without thought, Will leaned over and kissed her. A gentle, sweet kiss that broke into a passionate embrace when Cate, thanks to the scotch, responded wholeheartedly. Will's lips brushed across her teary cheeks, her neck, her shoulders, and back to her sweet mouth. His passion for her churned in his belly. She was so soft, so sweet, so lush.

"Shit." Will sat upright. "I'm sorry, sugar. I need to stop." What the hell was he thinking? He should leave. He should say this friendship was wrong. Against the rules. Was a dead end.

"Stop?" Cate slurred.

"I don't want you to have any regrets." *Like I already have.* He had taken another step further on the wrong side of the boundary line.

Cate shrugged.

Get up, ole boy. Get up and walk out now, the rational side of him shouted. *Why am I even here? Is it sex? Am I just a hound dog refusing to stay on the porch? The freshness of her innocence?* Will lived a life plodding through the muck of crime. Cate was a lone flower that had pushed through the crack in his cement heart.

Will hadn't always had the upper hand when it came to life's offenders. A short kid with a slight stutter made him an easy target. Until that last time, after being pushed into a locker and trapped until someone reported the banging, Will decided to do two things that changed the course of his life. First, he got speech therapy. And second, he found that egg-suckin' coward, jumped him from behind, and beat the living tar out of him.'

Yep, he sure as heck got suspended for breaking school rules, but from that day on, Will was respected.

Some rules we made to be broken.

"Why would I have regrets?" Cate mumbled.

"Aren't you and Edward exclusive?" Will asked, despising himself for what he was about to do.

Cate stared at the rug's delicate pattern and nodded.

"I mean . . ." Will hung his head and looked down at the carpet. "He doesn't see anyone else, does he?"

"No, Will. I get it. This was a mistake."

"It's just that I followed him after he left here tonight . . . and he went to Aurora Avenue."

"So?"

"He picked up a hooker."

"Why would you say something as mean as that?" Cate paled and sat up. "Oh, no—"

She vomited onto the carpet.

"Let me get you—"

Cate vomited again.

"The room is spinning." The slurring would have been cute had there not been all the gagging.

Will hurried into the kitchen, grabbed a wet towel, and came back to help clean the mess.

"I'm sick," Cate moaned.

"Wow. Two shots, huh?"

"I also had two before you came," Cate confessed.

"Do you feel you need to throw up again?" Will finished cleaning the carpet.

Cate shook her head.

Will grabbed the blanket on the back of the couch and wrapped it around Cate.

"Lie back, sugar," Will murmured. "I'll take care of you tonight."

CHAPTER 30

EDWARD JERKED AWAKE in a pool of sweat. He pulled himself off the sofa and took a moment to wake up. His nightmare was over, but Candy, the hooker he'd picked up the night before, was still in the middle of hers. Hog-tied, gagged, and stuffed in a storage area under Edward's house, she'd be Edward's plaything until he got bored. Since morning light was budding, he decided he'd keep her around for the day and then take her to her final resting place later that evening.

He walked into the den, rolled the pricey Turkish Oushak area rug just enough, lifted the trap door, and reveled in the horror hardened in Candy's eyes.

"What did you expect?" Edward told her. "Don't you know better than to get into cars with strangers?"

Candy struggled to speak, but the panties stuffed in her mouth made it impossible.

He pulled her out of the storage space and dragged her into the kitchen.

The phone rang.

Caitlyn. Again.

Serves her right.

"What is it with you bitches?" Edward kicked Candy. "Must." *Thud.* He kicked her again. "You." *Thud.* "Have." *Thud.* "Everything?" *Thud. Thud. Thud.* "Goddamn fucking whores, all of you."

He kicked until she stopped squirming. She'd either passed out or was dead. Edward didn't care either way. He hauled her back to the storage area, pushed her in, and shut the trap door.

THE NEXT MORNING, Cate had trouble concentrating. Last night's fight with Edward somersaulted in her mind like an annoying tune that kept repeating. She reread the doctor's orders for Mrs. Grayson three times before they sunk in. Twenty mg/kg IV *Vancomycin* every eight to twelve hours. Cate's head pounded as she dragged herself to the medical center's pharmacy.

She wasn't sure how many shots of scotch she'd had but knew it was enough to make her pass out last night and wake up with a hangover. And the fight with Edward . . . he'd jumped to conclusions, and Cate didn't blame him.

She had kept her friendship with Will a secret.

I had to.

Edward would have made a big stink about it, which he did. Cate had learned that when Edward didn't like something, it was easier to conform or to lie. When it concerned Will, Cate felt more comfortable with the lie.

And where had it gotten her? Her boyfriend thinks she's having an affair, but she isn't . . . *is she?* Her feelings for Will? Well, he was useful. Cate pried information about Ruby's murder and the Copycat from him with ease. He was loyal; when she needed him, he was there. And he was easy to manipulate. Is that what an affair was? She didn't know what love felt like. She understood *what* the word implied—after all, she loved her dad—but she never *really* understood the dynamics.

What she *did* feel was an inexplicable connection to Edward. Something deep in her resonated with him. It was strong enough to keep her interested even when he acted like a rabid dog. She had tried to reach Edward all day. Was he ever going to speak to her again? Perhaps, after work, she'd make a surprise visit.

Eager to leave, Cate watched the clock until her shift ended. She stopped at the hospital gift shop, picked up a colorful bouquet of balloons, and headed for Edward's house. When she arrived, the curtains were drawn, even the blinds in the garage window were closed. Cate parked on the gravel, grabbed the balloons, and rang the doorbell.

Nothing.

She thought she heard something move inside and rang again—still nothing.

Cate tied the balloons to the door handle and sat on the stoop. She tried to remember if Edward had mentioned any out-of-town business, but nothing came to mind.

How would she get out of the mess she'd created? The lie was explainable, but what about the kiss she shared with Will? The guilt sat on her like an oversized bully. *What about that?* She couldn't explain it to herself. The alcohol, Cate reasoned, was the real culprit. If she hadn't been upset, if she hadn't had the drinks, none of this would have happened. That's it. No more drinking with Will.

But in a way, this craziness was Edward's own fault. She'd told him, quite clearly, he wasn't the boss of her. No one was.

But.

Cate flashed on what Will had said about Edward. *On Aurora? With a prostitute?* Quick anger rushed through Cate. Why would Will say such a thing?

Cate grabbed her cell phone and called Will.

"Why did you follow Edward last night?"

"Good afternoon to you, too," Will replied.

"I'm serious. Why did you follow him?"

"I don't trust him."

"It's not your business," Cate snapped. "And then to make up stories for your own benefit. That's wrong."

"I didn't make up anything," Will shot back.

"You expect me to believe that Edward left my house and went to see a prostitute. That's not Edward."

"Or it *is* him, and you don't know him as well as you think."

Cate's phone clicked with another call.

"That's him. Gotta go."

She switched to Edward's call. "Hello?"

"Hello, Caitlyn," Edward said, his tone flat.

"I'm so glad you called. I've been a wreck." Cate stumbled on the words.

"I needed time to think things through."

"Will and I are just friends. I swear—"

"Why did you lie then?"

"Because I knew you didn't want me to be friends with him, and I didn't like you making restrictions on my life."

"He's a scum cop. He visits you for one reason. You don't understand how this kind of guy thinks. He comes sniffing around when I'm not there. I'm not an idiot."

"It's not like that at all." Cate thought back to the passionate kiss she'd shared with Will. "Why did you go to Aurora Avenue last night?" She hadn't planned on mentioning this, but it came out so quickly that her words seemed to blur.

"What?" Edward answered, his voice steady. "Aurora Avenue? What are you talking about?"

"Will followed you."

Edward laughed. "He's a lying asshole."

"Why would he lie?"

"Don't you see he's trying to put a wedge between us," Edward replied. "You *really* want to be friends with that prick?"

"Are you still mad at me?" Cate asked, avoiding answering the question about Will.

"How could I stay mad at you? And hey, I'm sorry I've been such a grouch. That's not the normal me. Just a little on edge." Edward fingered the small vial of cocaine in his jacket pocket. It clinked across the magnetite stone he always carried—*Keeps evil spirits at bay. At least, that's what the woman at the bookstore said.*

"When do you get off work?"

"I'm off. I'm at your house," Cate admitted.

"Ah, shit." Edward laughed.

The front door opened.

"How long have you been here?"

"I knocked and rang the bell." Cate stood up from the step, hugged Edward, and handed him the balloons.

"I must have been in the shower. Look, how sweet." He took the balloons and kissed her. "C'mon in."

While Cate and Edward chitchatted in the living room, Candy regained consciousness. No problem for Edward. Once he'd heard Caitlyn's car pull up to the house, he'd hurried to the den, climbed down to the storage area, blinded Candy, and bound her already gagged mouth with duct tape to be sure she'd stay quiet.

She did.

CHAPTER 31

CATE HAD JUST finished dinner at Edward's house and carried the dishes into the kitchen. She was relieved that bringing the balloons had worked and looked forward to a relaxing evening at Edward's.

"I guess you better head home before it gets too dark."

"I thought I'd stay over tonight."

Edward hesitated. "Did you feed Pipsqueak before you came?"

"Aw, gosh darn it. I forgot to stop at home."

Edward shrugged and handed Caitlyn her purse. "As I said . . ."

"Cheeses, Edward, are you trying to get rid of me?"

"Sure am." His laugh sounded hollow. "You know I have your best interests at heart."

MINUTES AFTER THE sound of Caitlyn's car heading down the road turned to quiet, Edward checked Candy, who was a shivering mess. He pulled her out of the storage area, dragged her to the shower floor, ripped off the tape that covered her eyes, and rinsed her with cold water.

Candy's eyes moved wildly. Sounds of terror came from her panty-stuffed, taped mouth.

"You trying to tell me something, honey?" Edward said with a malevolent smile. "Sorry, not in the mood for complaints."

Tears dribbled down her cheek and across the tape that sealed her mouth.

"Is crying all you bitches know how to do?" Edward lugged Candy into his kitchen and grabbed her neck. Still hog-tied, she squirmed on the Italian tile floor. Edward didn't flinch. He kept his determined hands gripped and squeezed until Candy's struggle finally subsided.

The creamy rush jolted through Edward as if he'd injected a cocktail of the best drugs he'd ever tried—heroin, cocaine, crack, meth, ecstasy, and more. He leaned back against the cabinet in s stupor.

And then reality broke him out of his daze.

How long had Will followed him? Long enough to see him drop the first hooker off? Did he wait the few hours Edward drove around until he'd circled back and picked up Candy? Edward shook his head. No, he would have seen Will's car lights when he drove the first prostitute up in the hills.

Now, Edward needed to deal with Candy. He waited until he felt under control, dragged Candy's limp body to the trunk, took an early morning ride, and dumped her alongside a trail on Taylor Mountain. After a stop at an all-night diner, Edward visited a bagel shop and picked up an assortment for the nurses on five-east.

Edward arrived on the fifth floor close to 8:45 that morning, and the nurses greeted him like a kaleidoscope of butterflies—all of them, including Scott, took turns flirting and flitting around him. One of them grabbed his hand and led him into the breakroom.

"Where's Caitlyn?" Still high from the kill, Edward's good mood was contagious.

"Who cares?" One nurse laughed.

"We'll keep you busy," said another.

Just then, Caitlyn walked into the break room. "I heard you were here." She kissed him on the cheek.

Edward could instantly tell that something was on Caitlyn's mind.

"What's new, bamboo?" Edward hugged her.

Caitlyn checked her watch. "Do you have to meet clients for lunch?"

"Sure do," Edward lied.

"I have a break in ten. Can you wait? I need to talk to you."

"Absolutely." He grabbed a magazine. "I'll be right here."

EVEN THOUGH IT was pouring, Caitlyn wanted to get out of the hospital during her break. She and Edward stood under the awning covering the hospital entrance. Because of the thunderstorm with its winter chill, others stood in the warm, dry lobby waiting for rides or a break in the rain to run to their cars.

"When does a Seattle detective carry an umbrella?" Edward asked.

Caitlyn shrugged. "Nobody local carries an umbrella."

"It's a joke," Edward said.

"Okay, when?"

"When he's undercover."

Caitlyn didn't laugh.

"Not funny?" Edward asked.

"One of my patients died," Caitlyn said.

"I'm sorry. Were you two close?"

"No, it's not that," Caitlyn replied. "Yesterday was a bad day. I mean, we had that argument, and I hadn't heard from you . . ." She wove her arm around Edward's. "I'm sure I gave Ms. Grayson the right medication. I checked it at least three times. It was an antibiotic, that's all. But she died later that day."

"Why did she die?"

"The antibiotic wasn't effective. We thought it was, but the meningitis overran the Vancomycin dose. No one has said anything, but I feel responsible. Maybe if I had paid more attention—"

"You *did* pay attention, Caitlyn." Edward turned to face her. The wind changed direction, and rain pattered on the awning. "You checked her dose three times. She didn't die until you'd already left work. She wasn't under your care."

Thunder rumbled in the distance, and the rain increased in intensity.

"Still—"

"Why do you always blame yourself? You care so much for your patients. There were plenty of variables. The dosage the doctor prescribed, her body's inability to fight off the disease. Shit, anything could have happened after you left."

The wind tilted, and a stream of rain hit Caitlyn.

"Aw shucks. Let's go back in," Caitlyn said. "I'm getting soaked."

"You okay about this now?"

"Not sure."

"Don't take this on. It's not your fault."

"I might look for another job," Caitlyn declared as though she'd just snapped out of a trance. "I don't like the environment at this hospital."

"But you're so well-liked here."

They stepped through the double-doors of the hospital and hurried in.

"No," Caitlyn said, pulling off her now-soaked sweater. "It's you they like."

CHAPTER 32

WILL HAD LEFT three messages on Cate's cell the morning after Edward had stormed out. At first, Cate chose not to respond. She didn't know what to say to him. Was Edward right? Was Will trying to break up their relationship? Will *did* kiss her. Yes, she had kissed him back, but that didn't count, did it? She'd been drinking, upset, and confused.

Will had lied to her. He *must* have. Edward with a prostitute? Impossible. Rich, handsome, and charismatic, Edward didn't have to pay for sex—especially for a girl on Aurora. That is if he wanted to cheat, which he didn't.

Did he?

They rarely made love. That was normal, right? And if he desired more, he had only to make a move. She couldn't imagine him being with someone else.

Even so.

A lingering flicker of doubt prompted the impulsive call to Will.

"I'M GLAD WE could meet." Will pushed his glass aside and scanned Tipsy's Cow Burger Bar for the waitress. "Where's my shake refill?"

"I can't stay long," Cate said.

"I know. I know." Will waved to the waitress. "Edward at eight."

"I've been thinking about what you said about Edward, and I need to know the truth."

"You still think I made that up?"

Cate's cell rang before she could respond.

"Shush." She turned her attention to the phone. "Edward." Her voice turned sugary sweet.

Will rolled his eyes, slid out of the booth, and shadowboxed.

Cate gestured, *one second*, and shot him a stern look, then forced lightness in her voice. "It's okay, I understand. Okay, tomorrow, then."

Cate was quiet a minute then shoved her cell into her purse. "He canceled," she said, her shoulders visibly drooping.

"Cate," Will breathed. "Maybe I was wrong. Maybe it wasn't Edward I saw on Aurora."

"That's what I thought too."

"Looks like you're free tonight, after all." Will smiled.

CHAPTER 33

WILL WALKED FROM Tipsy's to his car in a murky fog of regret. *Here I am pissing on my own leg and saying it's raining. Since when am I a scheming liar?* He shook his head. *But Caitlyn will end up with that bologna wrapper of a man if I play hardball. I see that now.*

Will drove up Aurora Ave. N. and slowed as he passed a cluster of prostitutes standing around the entrance of a seedy motel. *This is where that scumbag picked up the girl.* He pulled into the parking lot, grabbed a printout of Edward's DMV picture, and headed toward the girls.

"Hey, Will." A woman wearing short shorts, a striped see-through blouse, and high heels slinked over to him.

"What's up, Daisy?"

"Same shit, diff'ren day."

"I hear you."

"What brings ya over to my side of town?"

"Have you seen this guy picking up dates?" He handed her the printout.

"Why?"

"Just following up on a lead."

"Nah. Let me check with the girls." Daisy sauntered over to her group, who passed the picture around and handed it back.

Daisy returned with a younger woman in tow.

"Will, this is Clarise."

Clarise wore a black wig, too-heavy eyeliner, and lipstick that matched her painted-black nails. Her skin looked purple-pale. If vampires lived in Seattle, Will would have run for a clove of garlic.

Before moving to Seattle, Will had rented a condo in a repurposed warehouse close to the French Quarter in New Orleans. He often jogged on Bourbon Street—where, according to many—vampires liked to roam. Many nights, he'd run down empty streets, the only noise—the *thud, thud, thud* of his sneakers hitting the sidewalk. More than once, he'd see a shadow disappear into an alley or hear the fluttering of bats. Did Will believe in vampires? No. Did he carry garlic just in case? Yep. He wasn't a fool.

"Hey, Clarise." Will shook her hand. "You've seen this guy?"

"I had a date with a guy that looked like him."

"Did he give you his name?"

"Nah, just handed me twenty dollars and took me for a ride. He said he's had a fight with a girlfriend and needed to blow off some steam. I remembered him cuz he didn't want nothing from me. Dint say much. Just drived. We went to the woods. He drinked whiskey, offered me the bottle; we did coke, lots of it, and then he bringed me back."

"What kind of car? Color?"

"Big. Dark."

"Do you know what make?"

"Nah, I just remember the face. Clean-cut. Good-looking."

"Did he try to get rough with you?"

"Just drived and got high with me. A real gentleman."

"If you see him again, try to remember the car. Get his name. Memorize the license plate."

"That sounds like a lot of work," she said, her tone frosty.

Will reached in his pocket, pulled out a twenty, and handed it to her.

"Well, ain't you a gentleman too."

"Here's my card. Keep the picture and show it around."

Clarise stuck the card and twenty into her small purse and strolled back to the other girls.

Perplexed, Will headed back to his car. *Why the hell did Edward take the woman for a ride, get her high, and bring her back?*

CHAPTER 34

ONLY A WEEK had passed since Edward's blow up with Caitlyn. Although he'd refrained from seeing her—hell, he had to show her who had the control in this relationship—his nemesis had started badgering him.

Does the hassle ever end? the spiked creature squawked in circular repetitions. *Does it? Does it? Click-clack. Click-clack. Does it? Does it? Does it?*

As he headed out of Seattle, Edward glanced at The Darkness, who sat in the passenger seat like an obedient pet.

Trophy or not, is this woman worth it? I mean, come on, boss. I'm looking at this from a purely objective point of view. As Ruby would have said, "This is complete mishegoss," The Darkness clucked.

Oh, now you're speaking Yiddish? Go on, keep it up, Edward said.

You got to admit, it's a good word for craziness. Hey, look ahead. See that woman hitchhiking? I'll betcha you can't pass by without picking her up.

As if you already haven't been irritating me.

Edward drove toward the girl—*I'm just being kind*—pulled the car to the curb and motioned to the woman with her thumb in the air. *God only knows what kind of monsters travel this highway,* he thought with a smirk. He lowered the passenger window. "Looks like rain."

"Sure does," she said, looking up at the clouds.

"Where you headed?" Edward glanced at the sky. Like drugged horses, storm clouds lumbered toward Ellensburg—about two hours southeast.

"Boise." She looked at him as if appraising his clean-cut, all-American good looks. "You?"

"Vegas."

"Party town, ay?"

"Let me help you with that bag." He popped the trunk, got out of the car, and put the bag in.

"Thanks," she said, with a flirty-flirt smile. "I'm Allie." She pulled the door closed.

"I'm Edward." He pulled from the curb and back onto the road. "You from Canada, then?" Edward flirty-smiled right back. He'd been to Quebec and recognized the "ay" eastern Canadians said at the end of their sentences.

"I'm from Virginia." The woman twiddled a few strands of hair with her finger. "Moved to Quebec about three years ago."

She pronounced Quebec, Q-bay, which got on his nerves—just the teensiest bit. It reminded him of Americans who rolled their tongues when they said "Puerto Rico" as if they were suddenly Latino, as if they had the right.

"Speak French?" he asked, turning toward her.

"*Oui.*" The hitchhiker seemed relaxed and happy. "*Et vous?*"

"*Un peu.*" Edward stepped up the tête-à-tête. "So, ah, what's in Boise? School?"

He studied her. He liked her dark hair, her thin lips, her provocative neck. When she glanced out the window, the light scent of her perfume swirled in the car.

"Nope, not school," she said with a sultry smile. "Vegas, huh?"

"Taking a short holiday from law school."

"I thought about paralegal school." She became quiet for a long moment. "I took a break and never went."

"Do you know what lawyers wear to work?" Edward snapped a button on his armrest, and the doors locked.

"Well, that's—"

"A lawsuit."

"You're a real comedian."

The conversation progressed. She liked classical music. He liked alternative. She hated exercise. He hiked. She laughed at his bad jokes, and in return, he told more.

Edward was impressed with . . . *what did she say her name was? Had she said her name?* Impressed with *her.* He shot her a sideways glance. About an hour had passed since he'd picked her up. "Hey, you thirsty? I've got water in the back."

"Wow. Thanks," Allie said.

When they reached Snoqualmie Pass. Edward pulled off the road, handed her a bottle of water from a small cooler, and grabbed one for himself. "Like some French bread, champagne, and cheese? I've got great *fromage d'affinois.*"

It's going to start pouring," Allie said.

"Oh, no worries, we'll picnic in the car."

They took a fifteen-minute break to eat, and all the while, the creature hopped side to side in the back seat.

Back on the road. The sky had darkened, and the car struggled against rough wind. Trees reached with branch-shaped arms and muted thunder threatened. A flash of lightning, and seconds later, rain smothered the windshield.

Click-clack.

Edward ignored The Darkness.

The Darkness, sitting next to the cooler, opened its eyes. *Click-clack. Click-clack. Click-clack.*

Edward tried to speak over the clacking. "So, what did you say was in Boise?"

I was going to . . .blah . . . blah . . . blah . . .

Edward's teeth clamped together. The muscles in his jaw tightened. The click-clacking combined with the babbling of the girl to affect him like fingernails scraping slate. His palms dampened. His mouth parched.

Focusing its beady eyes on the girl, the creature jumped on Edward's shoulder, pushed its talons against his neck, and whispered, *Take her. You know you need it too.*

"No!" Edward said, although his body said yes.

"No, what?" Allie asked.

The shadow landed on Allie's shoulder and hunched his neck. It hissed then clacked his hooked beak open and shut. Open and shut. An oozing sensation filled Edward's groin. His heart pounded. The image of this Barbie-doll on the side of the road turned into a vision of her gasping for breath. The idea went from fantasy to need. Bad need. Have-to-have-it need.

Edward shrugged.

"I was heading down to see *mon ex-petit ami* but . . ."

Think about it. The Darkness' voice was like a siren luring a sailor off-course. *Better than sex. Better than coke. Better than any rush ever. Right, buddy?*

The woman prattled on. "But Vegas sure sounds fun—"

Fuck. As if I'd bring her with me, Edward thought. "I think we should pull over. The storm is too thick. Crap, I can barely see."

The large shadow pecked, and a sudden viciousness shot through Edward. He swerved the car off Route 90 and headed up a gravel road toward the trees. Cruelty clanged like an oversized cowbell. His lip curled just enough to show his teeth.

Edward couldn't stop the pressure building inside of him. All he could think of, the only thing that would satisfy him, was the rush of the kill.

"Where are we going?" Allie said.

Edward glanced at her but said nothing. His charismatic smile turned grim.

Click-clack. Click-clack. Click-clack. Click-clack.

"Edward?"

He heard her as if she were off in the distance—her words muted by the echoing of the click-clack spinning in Edward's mind.

"Where are you going? This doesn't seem right."

At that exact moment, the predator smelled her fear. The edge drove Edward. Made him crave the high.

"Let's wait on the side of the main road until the storm clears," Allie insisted.

Edward could tell she wanted to sound tough, but panic lined her words.

"Hey, *petit-pois* . . . why so sour?" Edward turned the charm back on.

"Because I don't want to get off the main road." She didn't sound so calm anymore. Allie wilted into the seat like a flower from a broken-hearted bride's bouquet.

The taste of her death rolled in Edward's mouth. He relished the terror in her eyes. Nothing compared to the control he felt, the sheer potency of a kill.

"I want out now." As if the girl had been shocked with a probe, she sat up straight and rebounded with a snarl.

Good for her, Edward thought. He liked spunk. "Hey, hey, hey, no worries," he said smoothly. "I know a shortcut."

"Stop. The car. Now."

Her firm tone brought a small laugh to Edward, which he chose not to suppress. The pungent smell of her distress was seductive.

"Here?" Edward kept driving. "Let me at least drive you to a—"

"Here," she screamed.

"Fine, then." He stomped on the brakes, and his Altima slammed to a stop. "You sure? Here?"

The sudden stop caused her to lurch forward and slam back against the seat.

"Now." Her scream level hit shrill.

Edward shrugged, "It's a long walk. I'll get your backpack from the trunk." He stepped out of the car and toward the back. He opened the trunk, got what he wanted, and was opening her door in seconds.

"Are you sure you want out? *Here?* This far from the highway. In the rain?" The gentleman had temporarily reentered Edward's psyche. Always a reassuring element. As if he was escorting her to a royal ball, he reached for her hand. "Can I at least take you to the highway? We'll go right this second. I know the back roads. This was a shortcut. You've got me all wrong."

"Let me go." She climbed out of his car. As soon as her feet hit the ground, she bolted.

Shit, in the rain? Is she going to make me chase her through the mud? Edward considered his new Louis Vuitton shoes. *Fuck.*

The girl had disappeared into the trees. Edward could hear her thrashing through the brush. He took off after her. The yellow of her rain slicker flashed in-between green bushes. He knew he could catch up in seconds. He didn't work that damn elliptical every day for nothing.

The girl screamed. Running and screeching as if the world was ending.

Fifty feet away.

"No! No! No!" she cried.

Edward kept coming.

"Somebody help me! Fire! Fire! Fire!" she yelled.

Thirty feet between them.

She was seconds away.

Twenty feet.

The girl tripped and lay there, gasping.

The Darkness circled like a hawk encloses its prey. Dipping then lifting again and again.

Edward fell on top of her. Usually, he saved the sex for after they were dead. But this one had ruined his shoes. He straddled her, held her arms flat against the mushy ground.

"Quit moving, shut up, and I won't hurt you."

The girl stopped squirming, and he opened his pants. He raped her, strangled her, revived her, strangled her—until he'd had his fun—and choked her until she made her final gasp. Finishing with a lovely lace ribbon tied around her neck, he then had sex with her—the right way.

Soaking wet and disheveled, Edward ran back to his car, jumped in, and headed back to the highway. The rain continued to pummel the roof of his car. Only keeping the windshield clear for a second, the wipers continued their monotonous swish-swash.

Edward congratulated himself for always having a piece of lace on him. Maybe when they write about him, they'll mention how organized and intelligent he is.

CHAPTER 35

BEING IN A RELATIONSHIP was a new concept for Cate. All the years she'd spent with herself—first studying in high school, then college, then getting her nursing degree and moving to Cincinnati. A private person, it had been difficult for her to maintain friendships—especially since she had a propensity toward leaving her job and moving.

Edward had opened a new world of possibilities for Cate. They went to jazz clubs, poetry readings, dancing. He even liked taking her to the eclectic boutiques sprinkled throughout Seattle's neighborhoods. Ruby had once told her, "If a man will go shopping with you, he's a keeper."

Ruby.

It had been almost six months since Ruby's murder, and still, the police had nothing except Jennifer Cannon's sketch. A face that could belong to hundreds of men. Heck, even Edward looked like the guy. Cate couldn't help but laugh, but then the reality of her life drew the curtains on her smile. For a second, she felt the black hole of pain locked in her heart.

Thank God she had Edward now. Could she have gone through Ruby's death without him? Who would have given her support? Who would have been there through all the tears? Who would have come over in the middle of the night when she'd heard noises in her backyard?

Will. That's who.

Cate tried to delete the thought from her mind, but it kept pushing its way to the front.

"I'M GLAD YOU called," Will said as he led Cate into his living room. A plush leather couch sat in front of the picture window with matching recliners on each side. A colorful blanket—looked African--laid on top of the sofa. Opposite the furniture, against the wall, hung a sixty-inch TV. The adjacent walls, painted terra cotta, were decorated with masks, spears, and artifacts from around the world.

"Wow. Your place is super." Cate set her purse on the rustic coffee table and sat on the ebony couch. "And could your TV be any bigger?"

"My friends and I are Mariners fans. I host the games when I'm not working." He lifted a framed picture from the coffee table and handed it to Cate. "That's Scott Servais and me."

"Oh," Cate said matter-of-factly. "How nice."

"Do you even know who he is?" Will set the picture back down and sat next to Cate.

"Nope." Cate laughed. "A Mariners' person?"

"The manager," Will said. "He's a friend."

"Wow!"

"Can I get you a drink? Sparkling water? Soda? Scotch?" He winked. Cate shook her head.

So, what brings this cup of sugar to my door?" he asked.

"I miss hanging out with you."

"Same here," Will replied. "Ok, Cate, I can see it in your eyes. What's going on in that little ole mind of yours."

"Do you like me?" Cate glanced at the out the window at the winter gray.

"Of course, I do." He scooted closer to her and took her hand.

"Edward says you are just using me. Is he right?" Caitlyn thought she saw a hint of anger in Will's eyes. "Don't be mad."

"Okay, sugar pie, I'll be honest. The guy's a jerk. What I know is that he lies—"

"But you said—"

"He lies, Cate. And he's possessive and controlling. But, he's right, I have what you call ulterior motives. I've got a crush on you bigger than the apple sign on Fred Pickerson's market."

"Oh, dear," Cate mumbled. "I meant—"

"I know what you meant," Will said and leaned in and kissed her. "Well, I guess that move was a mistake. A foul ball disguised as a home run. Lord, I shouldn't have done that," he mumbled.

"I didn't mind. Cripes, I kissed you right back."

"Yep, you sure as well did. But I'm risking my career."

"Why? Tampering with evidence?" Cate laughed.

Will put his hands to his head. "What in the good Lord's heavens am I doing?"

"No one will ever know," Caitlyn said. "It's in the vault."

"The vault?" Will lowered his hands.

"Information goes in." She pointed to her brain. "But I'm the only one with the combination."

Will considered Caitlyn's accidental slips when he'd confided in her in the past. He felt as nervous as a long-tailed cat in a room full of rockers. *What was this ole boy thinking?*

CHAPTER 36

"WHY ARE YOU with me?" Caitlyn asked Edward as he set up for a movie in his home theater. He was back from his adventure with Allie, three days now, but the chill from the rain that day seemed to have settled in his bones.

"I'm in love with you, that's why." Edward glanced up at her and flashed a perfect smile.

"Why?"

The Darkness, on top of a bookshelf, squawked. *Jesus. This constant need to analyze every Goddamn thing is what I'm talking about, partner.*

"I guess because . . ." *God, I hate this shit,* Edward looked at the creature that was now clattering its teeth. "You're open. Compassionate. I feel like I can be myself with you." *Well, no. But maybe I'll get up the nerve to share more . . . sometime.* "I love how you still adore your father, even after he killed . . . I mean, committed those crimes. The real question is, Why won't you marry me?"

"I'm kind of a loner. The thought of sharing my space with someone else makes me claustrophobic. I used to think of my . . . my father locked in a cell, and I'd fill with anxiety. Since then, I've kind of stayed to myself."

"Why are you with *me?*" *Do I even care?*

"Because of your sense of humor." Cate laughed.

"Why did the serial killer tell jokes?" Edward decided to test the water.

"Oh, Edward, please!"

"Because he wanted to take a stab at being a comedian." With that, Edward lunged across the room, landed on top of Caitlyn, and kissed her cheeks, her forehead, her chin, and her neck.

"This is why I love you," Caitlyn said between a chain of giggles.

Like your father? Edward thought. *Could you love me like that?*

CHAPTER 37

"SO, I RECKON I owe you an apology." Will handed Cate a pair of chopsticks and opened food containers lined across his coffee table.

"Whatever it is, I didn't notice, so no problem." Cate tried to hold the piece of sesame chicken between her chopsticks, but each time she got it close to her mouth, it dropped. "Gosh darn it, hand me a fork. I'll lose twenty pounds if I keep eating this way."

"I might as well just say it. Our boy, Edward, didn't have sex with the prostitute he picked up that night."

"I don't want to talk about this, Will. You know it's a sore spot."

"I thought you might want to know he didn't cheat. I mean, he took her for a ride, and they partied in the car, but no sex."

"So, you're still trying to convince me Edward picked up a prostitute. Why are you dwelling on this? You said it wasn't him. Edward's right, you're trying to drive a wedge between us."

Will dipped an egg roll into the hot mustard, twirled it in sweet and sour sauce, and set it back on his plate. "I don't have to drive a wedge between y'all, he's doing a good job himself. Is this what you think relationships are like? It's okay that he gets mad and disappears for days?"

"My dad was the same way. I guess I understand it."

"Your boyfriend is drinking and doing coke with hookers, Cate."

"Edward doesn't do drugs. He calls cocaine 'white poison.'"

"Jesus, Cate. Will you wake up? This guy's a liar."

"Stop. Do you hear me? Just *fucking* stop." Cate dropped her fork on her plate, stood up, and stormed out of the room.

"Cate. Cate!" Will followed her down the hall, grabbed her shoulder, and turned her toward him.

"Can't you let that all go?" Cate snapped.

"Don't you understand?" Will whispered. "I love you."

Cate stopped. "Wh . . . what?"

He brushed her hair away from her eyes and kissed her lips. Then again. Again. And again—until they stumbled into his bedroom, landed on his bed, and forgot about everything except for each other.

"YOU SAID 'FUCKING.'" Will sat up in bed and propped a pillow behind his head and shoulders.

"Huh?"

"You said, 'Just *fucking* stop.'"

"It's not funny," Cate pulled the sheet around her, caressed Will's chest, and burst into laughter. "You're right. What's gotten into me?" She blushed.

Will pulled Cate close and ran his hand through her hair. "I like your hair down. You look angelic."

"An angel who swears. Sorry about that." Cate became quiet. The only sound was the ticking of the clock.

A sense of dismay fled through Cate. Gosh. She had told herself she would not see Will again, and the minute he asked her to come over, she jumped at the chance. And now she'd made love with Will.

CHAPTER 38

A CRYSTAL, TULIP-shaped bowl held three turquoise-colored Ocean-breeze rose tops floating in the water. Candleholders held white-tapered candles. A path of the rose petals led from the living room to the bath where fragrant lavender candles surrounded a large freestanding tub with clawfoot legs. On the bed lay a gorgeous evening gown—high in the front, low-cut in the back—next to a set of 3-carat diamond earrings, silk stockings, and a pair of Jimmy Choo shoes. They'd be dining in tonight, and Edward wanted things just right.

Painted in stark white and surrounded by a wraparound porch, Edward's home was more majestic than Will's place. But the contrast was even sharper—inside, a sense of simplicity lingered in every element, including the furniture. Clean, crisp lines, a simple color palette, and the use of metal, glass, and steel gave the interior a sleek style. There were no paintings nor art on the white walls, and the place was clutter free.

The doorbell rang once. He let it ring again—proper decorum insisted on it. He swung the door open, and Caitlyn gave him an enormous hug.

"It seems like forever," Caitlyn said, happiness turning the corners of her mouth into a smile. She handed Edward a bouquet.

"Business has been crazy." Edward handed her a shot of Johnny Blue and took a double for himself. "Tonight, I make it up to you." He took her by the hand and led her through the kitchen where they followed a path of petals to his master bedroom then into the large bath.

"Edward. This is the most romantic thing I've ever seen."

"First, we relax," Edward said. He removed Cate's scrubs and lingerie and helped her into the tub. After adding rose and lavender oils to the water, he massaged her head, her hands, and her feet until she moaned her stress away.

"Wrap this around yourself." He laid a plush robe across the towel rack. "Your things are in the bedroom. Get dressed and meet me in the dining room in ten."

CATE TRIED ON the gorgeous dress that was modest yet sexy. And the diamond earrings. She grabbed them and went straight to the standing full-length mirror. She put the earrings on and moved into the bathroom to check them out in the magnifying mirror.

Cate appraised their spectacular sparkle. She had to admit, they looked smashing. She stood in front of the mirrored medicine cabinet. *Hmm . . .* the temptation to open the door and peek felt irresistible. Ruby had said, "If you don't want to be a nurse with a purse, judge a man by what's in his medicine cabinet."

Cate resisted the urge and returned to the gown. The material felt like satin and cascaded down her body like thick cream. She stepped into the matching pale pink heels and sashayed down the hallway to meet Edward in the dining room.

Edward stood near the set table in a sharp tux. He let out a low whistle. "What a knockout."

"You like?" Cate swirled in a circle to show off the dress. She was Rose from *Titanic*, Scarlet from *Gone with the Wind*, Katie from *The Way We Were*.

"Mm-hmm." Edward walked over to Caitlyn and took her into his arms. "May I have this dance, Ms. Derry?" He clicked the remote, and piano notes from "Mariage d'Amour" floated into the room like the intro to a romantic movie scene.

Cate allowed herself to fall into Edward's embrace. This moment, right here, was why she felt so deeply about Edward. As he held her, she could feel his strength, his sturdiness, his power, and his sense of control. And she reveled in how safe it was to be in his arms. She never, ever, ever wanted this moment to end.

First, they ate dinner, then clinked a toast in the hot tub, picked out shapes in the stars, and made sweet love. After, Cate headed to Edward's room to throw on her PJs. He stayed behind to bring the dinnerware into the kitchen. As soon as she walked into the master bath, she tumbled from her afterglow when she noticed the medicine cabinet door was slightly ajar. It was almost as if it were begging her to just peek one time.

No harm in that.

Edward seemed to know everything about her. What was wrong with doing the same?

She opened the cabinet door a little farther and took a glimpse. A toothbrush, toothpaste, razor, shaving cream, hair mousse, Rogaine (*aw . . . how cute*), three prescription bottles, Advil, a thermometer. Cate turned away then glanced back to the prescriptions. Half a container of prednisone, some Vicodin, and a container filled with four white rocks in a pile of white powder.

Cate opened the clear, orange-tinted bottle, stuck her pinkie in the powder, and dabbed a small amount onto her fingertip. *Heroin? Meth? Cocaine?* White crystals glittered. *Do I dare? Of course, I do.* She rubbed the light film of powder inside her nose, which went numb.

Cocaine.

Holy cathedral, Edward has cocaine.

"Hey," Edward called down the hall. "Where's the guest of honor?"

Cate didn't know what to say. She wanted to ask him about it but didn't want to risk ruining the night. But it was already a bust . . . at least for her.

Cate walked out of the room.

AS SOON AS Caitlyn came into the living room, Edward already knew something was up. She wore her PJ bottoms and a bra.

The Darkness adjusted its wings and *clacked* twice.

Stop it, Edward said.

Click-clack. Click-clack.

Edward glanced at Cate again. "What's wrong?"

"Do you lie to me?" Caitlyn stared past Edward as if trying to find an entrance to another world.

"Christ. It's that asshole again. I told you to stay away from him. Why don't you listen to me?"

"It wasn't Will." She held out the container.

The Darkness shot across the room and landed next to Edward on the couch. *Click-clack, click-clack, click-clack, click-clack.*

"So?" Edward stood up and headed for the scotch.

As if this were hilarious, The Darkness strolled to the coffee table alongside Edward with his beak clamped together. It was obvious he trying to keep from breaking into hysterics.

Edward slammed two doubles. Then picked up the bottle and drank the rest.

"This is cocaine, Edward."

Edward faked a laugh. "What? Cocaine?"

"I put it in my nose."

"I don't know what it is. I've never seen that before." He took the container, opened it, snorted, and then said, "It's cocaine, all right."

"Are you using cocaine? You lied to me?"

Caitlyn just stood in her bra and pants, and her neck . . . her long, slender neck . . . Edward gritted his teeth and threw the open container across the room against the coffee table. The Darkness hopped around, pecking at Edward's leg.

"It's not mine."

"Really, Edward? How naïve do you think I am?"

Pretty damn naïve, thank God. "Is this your idea of a sick joke?" Edward said. "Will put you up to this."

"We both know it's yours." Caitlyn's frustration filled the air.

"It's not."

It was in your medicine cabinet.

"Nope, never have seen it before."

"So, you're saying you never noticed this?"

"You were snooping?"

"No . . . I mean . . ."

"Fine, Caitlyn. Just fine. If you don't trust me, what's the point?" He grabbed his keys, opened the front door, and slammed it on his way out. Across the porch, down the steps—he got to his car.

Caitlyn ran after him. "I just need to know," she yelled from the driveway.

"Stop trying to catch me doing something I don't do." Edward backed up the car and screeched out of the driveway.

CATE WATCHED EDWARD burn rubber as he raced down the long road that led away from his estate. She tried his cell, but it went to voice mail. *I rushed to judgment,* she thought. *Could it have been in his cabinet, and he hadn't noticed? Was it his house cleaner's, and she'd forgotten? Why did he turn and run? Why does he always abandon me when he's upset? But that's what men do, right? That's what Daddy did when he was angry. He escaped by drinking himself into oblivion. He might as well have gotten up and left."*

Cate returned to the bedroom, put the diamonds on the bed, laid the dress next to them, and took some time to wrestle with her doubts.

EDWARD RETURNED THREE hours later. The table was still set, the clothes were laid out nicely, and Caitlyn was gone. *At least she blew out the candles*, he thought. He ended up in the kitchen where the now empty prescription bottle sat. *All that coke, gone.*

> Dear Edward,
> I hate that you leave when we need to talk.
> I tried to call you over ten times. Why didn't you answer?
> I'm sorry I overreacted. Please forgive me.
> Cate

Edward had to hand it to her; even when she was upset, she was still a lady. He grabbed the container and headed to the living room to search for the rocks.

CHAPTER 39

EDWARD PULLED AWAY from the curb and headed north on Aurora. Sugar, the twenty-something hooker he'd just picked up, sat in the passenger seat. She was quiet. Fiddled with her fingers. Licked her lips.

"Your first time?" Edward took the girl's hand and patted it.

"How did you know?" Sugar replied.

"I'm a criminal defense attorney. I need to size people up."

"That's so lit."

She seemed to relax.

Shit, the "attorney" bit was a home run. Edward's laugh added to his charisma. "Lit?"

"You know, awesome, cool. I'm studying to be a marine biologist. I've got goals AF."

What the hell is "goals AF"? Already, she was irritating him. "What's a gorgeous woman like you doing on Aurora? With your looks and class should be charging $250 an hour. I should hook you up with some people I know."

"That would be rad." *Blah, blah, blah, blah—*

In the backseat, The Darkness broke into a cackling laugh. *I'll bet you won't even make it out of town before you escort this one to the river. You getting salty?*

"Salty?" Edward muttered.

"Me?" Sugar turned toward Edward. "Nah, I'm in a great mood. Hey, dude, where we going?"

Edward kept driving; his eyes focused ahead. They were already on the outskirts of Seattle. He turned off the main street onto a dirt road and weaved up the hill into the woods.

"Dude, where are we?"

Edward reached a deserted campsite. He pulled off the road and clicked off the headlights.

"What do you want me to do?" Sugar scanned her surroundings. There was no moon glowing in the empty sky. "I'll do whatever you want. I mean, within reason. I'm new at this and—"

He slapped her face hard. "Will you shut the fuck up for two seconds? Jesus."

"I don't do pain. I don't want to—"

He grabbed her, choked her to unconsciousness, and then lifted her out of the car.

When she came to, she was flat against the top of a picnic table. Her hands and feet tied. She tried to speak, but Edward took care of that in a flash. He stuffed her panties into her mouth—*shut the fuck up.*

The Darkness sat in a tree clicking away. To add incentive, it squawked millennium slang. "Lit. OMG. Salty. Fleek. Lit. OMG. Salty. Fleek." *Click-clack. Click-clack.* On and on, like a broken carousel.

Rage soared through Edward, and he punched the girl on the side of her head. Punched her belly. Punched her face. Punched her chest. And choked her until her millennial eyes were lightyears away.

CHAPTER 40

THE SECOND WILL walked into work, LaKeisha approached him.

"Hey, Cambrey, that body the hikers found? Sarah Bloom." She patted Will's back. "Her finger was missing a ring she always wore."

"So, he's collecting trophies."

"Exactly. You got a message. 'The guy was seen on Aurora last night,'" she said, making quotation mark gestures in the air. "What's up on Aurora?"

"I've got nothing." Will walked over to his desk and pulled out the chair. LaKeisha took a seat facing him.

"What 'guy' is she talking about?"

"It's personal."

"Oh, really," LaKeisha said. "How about lunch? You can tell me all your secrets."

Well, damn, is LaKeisha flirting with me? The rumor that's she's an ice queen goes down the drain. "And you'll tell me yours, right?"

"I'll show you mine if you show me yours first."

"A friend thinks her boyfriend's seeing hookers. That's all."

LaKeisha leaned forward. "Special Agent Mills says lace ribbons link the Copycat with murders in Utah, Nevada, and Oregon. There might be a couple in Idaho. The FBI in Utah confirmed the info a half-hour ago."

"Holy shit. This guy's all over the place."

"So? What about lunch?"

"I've got a ton of paperwork," Will said. "How 'bout we order pizzas."

Will returned to his desk, sat down, and in seconds, his guilt about sleeping with Cate slapped him across the face. *Great job, jerk.* He let the thoughts steamroll through his mind. *I'm lower than a snake belly in a wagon rut. Sleeping with Cate.* He knew she was in a relationship. He knew he could lose his job. One phone call from Edward to the captain would end his career. He had to git out of this spiderweb, but how? When it came to his recent decision-making skills, he felt like a BB rattling in a boxcar.

FINISHED WITH HIS paperwork and lunch with LaKeisha, Will took a ride down to Aurora. After scanning the street with no luck, he pulled into the closest parking lot. He stepped out of his unmarked police car and rounded the building to the front of the motel.

Clarise, leaning into the passenger window of some john's car, looked annoyed when she saw Will.

"Sorry, buddy." Will escorted Clarise from the window. "She's already taken."

"What the fuck?"

As the green sedan pulled from the curb, Will handed her two twenties. "I've got you covered."

Clarise grabbed the cash and stuck it in her purse.

"What have you got for me?" Will glanced at other girls leaning in cars.

"I seen the guy yesterday night. He picked up a new girl."

"Is she here tonight?"

Clarise scanned the street. "Nah, dint see her. She mighta just been passing through."

"Did you see her come back last night?"

Clarise shook her head.

What time did you stop working?

"Around two this morning."

Did you get the make or license plate?

"Damn, sorry. I was high."

CHAPTER 41

CATE CAME HOME to a large bouquet of red roses on her front porch. She scooped them up and carried them in. Maybe Edward had cooled down. She had. After setting her purse on the chair, she took off her jacket, placed the vase of roses on the coffee table, and picked up Pipsqueak. It felt good to flop on the couch after a day filled with errands. She cuddled with Pipsqueak and opened the card: I'll be there at seven with Chinese. Edward.

She'd had Chinese last night with Will. *Oh dear, Will.* Her day off had been so hectic, she hadn't thought about him. Well, she hadn't *let* herself. If she had, thoughts of her time with him would have consumed her—his whispered words, his promises, his kisses, his touch. She could *not* see him again. How could she have let this happen?

Cate brought her palm to her forehead. *What have I done? I made such a stink about the cocaine . . . and I'm the cheat and liar.*

"CAITLYN?" EDWARD TAPPED her on the shoulder. "Hey, busy day?"

Caitlyn opened her eyes. "Oh, Edward. I must have dozed off." She glanced at her watch. "Geez, it's seven already."

"Some watchdog." Edward laughed and petted Pipsqueak. "I've missed you. I'm sorry I stormed out. It's difficult. After six months, you still don't trust me."

"I know. I'm so sorry."

"No, I am. I realized the coke was Lydia's. She does a great job with the house, but she has some questionable hobbies. Occasionally, I find a bottle of pills, an empty gin bottle, whatever. But who am I to judge? The house is always spanking clean."

"Did she snort coke with you?"

"*Seriously*, Caitlyn? After what we just went through, you ask me that?"

"Why didn't you stick around and talk about it?" Cate grumbled.

"Was I supposed to?" *Is that what you do when you fight with your girlfriend?*

"Well—"

Oh, Jesus. No wonder I've avoided relationships.

Click-clack.

Edward tried to ignore his insatiable shadow.

Click-clack.

"You're suffocating me with all the tears and distrust."

Suffocating—you're the expert, right? The Darkness chuckled.

"I'll try to be better. I'm just so new at this," Caitlyn replied.

"Not to worry." Edward handed her a small present. "For you."

"You don't need to—" She examined the gold box.

"Oh, yes I do. Open it."

"My gosh."

Edward had picked out an emerald-cut, 4-carat diamond ring.

"I don't know what to say." Caitlyn held the stone under the light. "It's beautiful."

Edward got on one knee. "Caitlyn, will you marry me?"

Silence bounced from wall to wall to wall like an out-of-control racquetball. It was in that grueling moment Edward realized two things: that she hadn't said yes nor was she looking him in the eye. *What's going through her mind? Does she think I don't love her?* He smiled. *I never got the whole love thing. Christ, just faking it is a hell of a lot of work. But I'll do what it takes to make her mine. Goddamn. Patrick Derry's daughter will soon be my wife.*

"I can't believe—"

"Is that a yes?" He sat next to her on the couch. *What the hell is this? I've morphed into the goddamn man of her dreams. She's crazy about me.*

Click-clack.

"Caitlyn?"

"It's not that I don't love you."

Click-clack. Click-clack.

"I just need more time." She shook her head and handed the ring back to Edward. "It's not you. It's me."

The Darkness pretended to gag. *Did she really just say that?*

Blinded by rage, Edward heard nothing except loud clanging in his head. Thinking became impossible. His fingernails dug into his palms. *Caitlyn, sitting there on her goddamn royal throne. What the hell is going on?*

He pulled Caitlyn from the couch. "It's that shit, Will, isn't it?" He grasped her shoulders and shook her. "Isn't it?"

"Edward, you're hurting me."

He read a flash of thrill in her eyes.

Edward grabbed her arm, dragged her into the bedroom, threw her onto the bed, and was on top of her in seconds. His straight arms kept his upper body elevated. "What do you think Southern Man will think when you tell him your Maddie story? Your father was a serial killer. Then you let your sister die? What's he going to think about that?"

Take it. Take her life. Now. Now. Click-clack. Click-clack. Click-clack.

Just as Edward positioned himself to make the kill, Caitlyn blurted, "You're not the boss of me."

Edward's rage crashed not into her childish words but the power behind them. He suddenly stiffened. "What did you just say?"

"I said, 'You're not the boss of me.'"

Thrown off-guard, he broke into wild laughter, rolled off her body, and then began to sob. *What the hell?* He gasped and force-stopped the tears. *He had almost lost control. Almost killed Patrick Derry's daughter. Almost got lost in a meltdown.*

He snapped his focus toward the entity, who bobbed its head up and down as it sat on the rim of the footboard. Still grinding its beak and snorting, The Darkness spread its wings and flapped to the dresser.

This is your fault, Edward snarled at the beast. *You broke our deal.*

Kiddo, you did this one yourself.

"Edward? Are you okay?" She sat up and shook his shoulder. "I think you had a seizure or something. We need to get you checked out." She got off the bed and grabbed her cell phone. "I'm calling 911."

"No, I'm fine." He grabbed her phone before she had a chance to call. "It's nothing. It just brought up something from my childhood," he lied.

"Want to talk about it?" Cate sat on the edge of the mattress and took Edward's hand as he scooted back and sat up.

He wasn't sure how he should act. Sad? Happy? Concerned? Instead, he said what always made things calm down. "I love you, Caitlyn Derry."

"I love you too."

CHAPTER 42

THE ONLY REASON investigators linked the body to the Copycat was the lace ribbon found on the ground a few feet from her body. Will examined the photographs and then dropped the file on his desk. The killer had beaten Clarice until her teeth had broken, her nose had collapsed, patches of hair had been ripped out, and her skull had cracked. But strangled?

No.

It was clear to the Seattle's FBI and police detectives that a different level of fury had triggered the Copycat Killer. Was this the same guy who killed the Ruby Valin? Was he losing control?

Will couldn't help but think he'd led the killer to Clarise. Maybe he'd been spotted talking to her. Maybe Clarise paid the price for his negligence? Was he barkin' up the wrong tree when it came to Edward? Or was Edward involved in Ruby's death? Did Edward know Clarise? After all, he did frequent Aurora Avenue.

Will watched LaKeisha grab her raincoat, hat, and umbrella and head toward the precinct doors.

"Keisha," Will called. "Where you headed?"

"Over to Green Lake. Wanna come?"

"Checking something out?"

"Nah, I like blowing off steam doing that three-mile walk around the lake."

"Leave the umbrella," Will said.

"It's drizzling." LaKeisha dropped her keys in her pocket.

"You'll stick out like a horse in a henhouse."

"Whatcha talking about?"

"The locals don't use umbrellas."

"*Seriously?*"

"Windbreaker and hat." Will thought back to when he first got to Seattle and tried to keep a low profile. His team laughed hysterically whenever he opened his umbrella. It took six weeks until someone finally told him to ditch the umbrella, get a windbreaker and hat, and learn to love the mist. He still wasn't used to the rain on his face, but hell—when in Rome.

HALFWAY AROUND GREEN Lake—past the giant sequoias, the bald cypresses, the elm trees, and oaks—LaKeisha grabbed Will's hand and lead him down a small sand area with a stunning view.

"How hard does a girl have to work?" LaKeisha still held Will's hand.

"I'm not sure what you're asking," Will replied.

"Can't you tell I've been flirting with you the last few weeks?"

Will felt the heat flush his face. Yes, he knew it. "I've been distracted lately."

"Are you interested in dinner sometime?" LaKeisha glanced across the lake where two kayakers paddled in the drizzly mist.

Will took a moment. "I'm sort of off the market these days, Keisha. Anyway, it's against policy."

"Damn! How embarrassing. I know I was stepping over a boundary. I'm sorry. Asking you to compromise your standards."

"Don't get me wrong. You're as pretty as a peach. If I didn't have my head so far up my ass, I'd be having dinner with you tonight." Will reconsidered LaKeisha—her cocoa-colored skin, dark hair tinted red, and voluptuous figure. She was shorter than Will but not by much. And a great person to talk to. They'd been having lunch off and on and had become good friends.

"What's up, Will? You can talk to me."

Will shrugged.

"What's bothering you?"

"That last body we found was Clarise Renault. I knew her. She kept a lookout for any girls who left with johns and didn't come back. Jesus. He shook his head. "Maybe he saw me chatting with her." A deep silence enveloped him.

"Did she have info for you?"

"Not really."

"If he beat her after he saw you talking to her, it points to him frequenting the Aurora area. Most of the recovered bodies have circled Seattle—his comfort zone."

They stood on the sandy shore and breathed in the mist.

"How could a place so beautiful harbor such a monster?" LaKeisha murmured.

For a moment, Will took LaKeisha's hand. "We'll get this guy."

"Shit, I wish had my umbrella," LaKeisha complained.

Will pulled her hood down to her brows. "That's how you do it."

LaKeisha stood up. "Let's get this trek over with."

CHAPTER 43

EDWARD SAT IN his sunroom and stared at the mist that veiled the trees. On his shoulder, The Darkness slept—its need to kill spent. Edward got up, walked into the kitchen, and opened and closed the refrigerator door. He paced back to the sunroom then down the hall to the screening room where he clicked on the TV and sunk into a recliner. The entity rustled as if waking but stilled right away.

Three days had passed since he'd proposed to Cate. Since then, an uncomfortable restlessness churned in his gut and burned through his veins like bootlegged whiskey. *What the fuck*; he stood up, threw the remote across the room, and headed back to the kitchen. His anger made sense, but the sobbing? *Because I was laughing so hard. That's all.* So why was he so unnerved?

It was that goddamned, shiny-headed, interloping cop.

The entity stretched its thorny wings, lifted from Edward's shoulders, and flew to the bar. *What y'all waiting for?* The Darkness let its words slide into an overdone southern accent. *Let's take him on a trip he ain't coming back from.*

Edward threw a roll of paper towels at the shadowy creature. *Oh, now there's a bright idea. Let's kill a cop and hang around town until they find us.*

You're the brains behind this operation. Let's hear your smart ideas. The creature paused. *No? Oh, that's right, you don't have any.*

"Wait a minute." Edward grabbed a bottle of Johnny, poured the scotch into a Glencairn Glass, and flopped into his reclining chair. On the TV screen, the words "Breaking News" flashed. They'd found the body of a hooker beaten to death, a lace ribbon around her neck.

Edward sipped the alcohol, took a hit off his vape pen, and watched her covered remains be carried on a stretcher and slid into a nondescript van.

Your right, Edward said. *We've got to get rid of that fucker.*

SINCE SHE'D BEEN working in Seattle, Cate had never called in sick. But for the last three days, she stayed home to cry. Her puffy eyes, rimmed in red, made her face look as if she'd been stung by bees. The hand-shaped bruise on her arm didn't ache as much as her feelings for Edward did. She'd never seen him this furious. Why had she told him she needed more time? Because of Will? Sure, she liked him—they had a good time. But the bottom line? She didn't care about him—he was a cop for goodness' sake. It was Edward that interested her, and even though he had a few walls, she connected with his underlying needs.

Cate glanced at her cell phone and willed it to ring. Why hadn't Edward called? He owed her an apology, right? It was *his* job to make that first step. He'd shaken her, dragged her down the hall, thrown her on the bed.

Although, she did know that his imprisoned emotions manifested as anger. And even if he could be unpredictable, getting him upset always served a purpose. When he was consumed with rage, Edward loved her enough to show the ferocity of his feelings. It was his form of intimacy.

Had she said no to his proposal to manipulate him? To get him riled up? To make him need her more?

Yes.

CHAPTER 44

"ALTHOUGH HE WAS killing in other states, they were relatively sure he was not just passing through Seattle. Most of Patrick Derry's victims were found in the Seattle area too. This is his comfort zone, but he travels. A string of bodies has been discovered along highways leading to Vegas; when the opportunity presents itself, he kills.

"He was in a rage when he picked up the Clarise Renault, beat the shit out of her, and dumped her near the airport. Maybe because he saw Detective Cambrey talking to her, maybe not. But the guy is starting to spin out of control. This is when he'll make mistakes." Agent Mills scanned the group of detectives and cops sitting around the room.

"Let's review what we've got? About six feet, medium weight, and white. He's in his thirties. Good-looking. Strong, probably works out. Possibly belongs to a gym. Maybe part-time worker, unemployed, or student. Travels to Las Vegas—something keeps bringing him back there. But he's local. Has been to Aurora and picked up girls. Not all the vics were prostitutes, though. Mostly not. We think he's an opportunist. When the urge hits, and there's no one else, a hooker is a sure thing."

"We know he prefers twenty to thirty-five-year-olds, but he's killed a lot older and younger. He knows off-road areas—so again, probably local," Will added.

"We should do another press conference," Captain Thorten said. "Get him agitated. Work him into a rage and then monitor Aurora. Get license plate numbers and types of cars."

"How about the witness?"

"Miss Cannon refuses to be in the public eye," Cambrey replied.

"What about the daughter?" LaKeisha said. "She must have insights—the Copycat is acting out her father's crimes.

"Derry's daughter?" Thorten asked.

"Nah, not a good choice," Will blurted. He felt his face heat up. "What I mean, after interviewing her, I don't think she'd be open to it."

"That's it! We'll have *her* address the Copycat during the press conference," Mills said. "I mean, goddamn, she's the Lace Ribbon Killer's daughter."

"Let me talk to her," LaKeisha offered. "Woman to woman."

"I'll do it," Will said. "We've had several conversations about her father. I think she trusts me."

"Okay, let's set it up as soon as Will talks to . . . What's her name?

"Derry," LaKeisha said. "Caitlyn Derry."

CHAPTER 45

HELD HOSTAGE BY his insecurities, Will sat in his car outside Cate's house. The last time he'd seen Cate was in his bed—and later that evening, Cate had texted:

Cate: We shouldn't have done that.

Will: I know.

Cate: I can't see you anymore. It was a mistake.

Will: I'm glad it happened, though.

Cate: Yes. I've got to go. He's in the next room.

Will: Can we meet to talk?

Cate: No. I have boundaries now.

When he had gotten the text, Will had felt like throwing the phone across the room. If she only knew what a pig-in-the-mud sleaze Edward was.

Will leaned back in the front seat and closed his eyes. Once again, he reviewed the facts that he'd noted. Clarice was a hooker from Aurora. Ruby was killed the same way. Sarah Bloom worked at the hospital where Edward visited Cate.

Was it a coincidence Edward was dating the Lace Ribbon Killer's daughter? Something was off about that guy . . . Could it be that he's a killer?

Will checked his watch. 1:45 p.m. The sun argued with rain clouds, and the streets were drizzly wet. *This is not a social call,* he reminded himself. *I'll say hello. State my business. Thank her and get out.*

Will popped the car door handle and plodded to the front door. His stomach gnawed. Beads of sweat formed on his brow. *Jesus, it's not like I'm walking to the hangman's noose.* He wiped his forehead with his sleeve and rang the bell.

Cate opened the door. "Hello, Will." Her fingers trembled slightly.

Knowing Cate, she'd looked through the peephole first, which was good. The element of surprise would not have been in his favor.

"I thought you'd respect my boundaries." Cate didn't look him in the eye; instead, she focused on his mouth.

"It's not what you think," he replied. "I'm here on official business."

"Like what?"

"Like you helping us catch the Copycat Killer."

Cate moved aside and motioned for Will to come in.

"Mind if I have a seat?" Will asked.

"You don't need to be so formal. You're here. You're in the house. Who are we kidding?"

"Right. Right." Will sat in a chair catty-corner from the couch. "Is Edward around?"

"No. Why?"

"I know it hasn't been that long, but I miss you something fierce."

"What about the Copycat?"

"The team has updated his profile, and the FBI wants us to hold another press conference."

"And?" Cate crossed the room.

"We want to lure him in. We think he's close to town. If you take the podium and make a plea to him, you know, mention your father, the team believes that boy will pitch a fit and make a mistake."

"You want me to go on TV and tell the world who I am? *And* use me as bait?" Cate sat down on the couch. "What about me? Did it ever occur to 'the team' that I'd be humiliated? That I'd be putting my life on the line?"

"I fought the idea, but the higher-ups call the shots. Aw, Cate." Will moved next to her on the couch. "I want you in my arms. Let me love ya, darlin', if just for today."

"Please stop," Cate muttered. "This is hard enough as—"

With the sweetest kiss he'd ever given, Will stopped her mid-sentence. He felt Cate relax into the kiss and embrace him back. Without a word, he lifted her, carried her upstairs to her bedroom, and made love to her as only he could.

"YOU'RE THE MOST fetching woman . . ." Will leaned toward Cate and propped his weight on his elbow.

Cate rolled to her side and faced Will. "So much for boundaries." She shook her head and smiled. She sat up and leaned against the headboard. "So, about the press conference."

"Before you say no—think about saving women's lives. Since he's duplicating your dad, he'll take a keen interest in you." Will brushed a stray hair away from her face. "You might-could-be the squirrel that brings the nut to the tree nest."

Cate thought of the nurses on five-east—*the covert staring at me as if I were a freak. The rumors. Would they think I'm the one who killed the patients? After all, it's in my blood. Of course, they would. I'd never be trusted again.*

But Will's right. Coming forward could cause him to make a mistake. He wouldn't want to kill me, not if he idolized my father—and all the women I'd help if they caught him. That's why I became a nurse. To help people. This is no different.

Let the damn nurses talk about me. They already do.

CHAPTER 46

EDWARD COULD NOT believe what he was seeing—on every goddamn channel, Caitlyn stood at a podium surrounded by cops. He could see the prick cop off to her side.

"Hello," Caitlyn said, a slight quiver in her voice. "My name is Caitlyn Derry. I am the daughter of Patrick Derry, the Lace Ribbon Killer. I'd like to direct my comments to the Copycat Killer. If you are anything like my father, you'll be watching this—just like my father watched the police hunt for him." She cleared her throat and took a sip of water left for her on the podium.

"This is a weird thing to say, but I loved my father. Yes, he was a monster and despicable out in the world, but I knew his other side. He was a good father and loved me."

"Right," Edward said to the TV. "Like Derry could feel love."

"I know you have another side too."

Edward turned off the TV. "Son of a fucking bitch." He threw a Franz table vase across the room and watched it crash against the wall.

Within seconds, the evil beast clawed into Edward's back.

What the fuck is she doing?" Edward said.

Looks like "someone" talked your girl into getting the Copycat to act out, the shadow replied. *Nice job, right?*

What do they think I'd do, go after her?

Want to?

Cut the crap, Edward snapped. *Fuck it!"* He grabbed his jacket. *Let's go have some fun.* The shadow followed close behind.

CHAPTER 47

THE PHONE CALL from Jennifer Cannon caught Will by surprised.

"I've moved to Bellevue. Got Fierce, my new Doberman pup. Have a different job." Her voice had a new strength to it.

"That makes me might happy." Will felt genuine joy for her. She was moving on. A survivor.

"So anyway, I was in Nordstrom today, and they gave out cards with cologne spritzed on them. That's when I smelled it. The scent the man who attacked me wore."

"Did you get the name?"

"Yes, it's Tonka 25."

"This is fantastic, Jennifer." Will glanced at the station's wall clock. 9:15 a.m. The mall opened at ten.

"Anything else?"

"That's it."

"If you come up with anything, you be sure to call."

"Will do, Detective Cambrey."

Cambrey ended the call and motioned to LaKeisha.

"What's up?"

"Want to take a ride to Nordstrom? I've got a lead. Small, but it's a new angle."

"I'm on it. Let me finish up a report, and I'll be ready to roll."

"I CAN'T BELIEVE you bought that cologne. You must have money to burn." LaKeisha sniffed her wrist as they headed from the mall to the car.

"You've got to admit you've never smelled anything like it. It's edgy. Dark. I like it."

"It's sexy, but then that could just be you." LaKeisha winked. "Me? I'd rather have that pair of Dolce & Gabbana shoes."

"Those pink ones?"

"Yep."

"$1145 for shoes?"

"Yep."

"You'd be taller than me."

"Take me out. I'll wear flats."

"Tonight, I'm heading over to Aurora. See if any of the girls recognize the scent?"

"Want company?"

A TWENTY-SOMETHING hooker looked worn out and hardened. If Will hadn't known better, he'd have guessed she was in her late thirties. He knew how the streets sucked the life out of these girls—mostly runaways— who'd tried drugs one time too many and now traded their souls chasing the dragon.

Will and LaKeisha approached a girl that Will had often seen on the streets but didn't know well.

"Hey, sweetheart," Will said to the brassy redhead whose heavy black eyeliner and extra-long false lashes competed with her skirt that was so short her rear cheeks showed. "Seen Daisy tonight?"

Whether they knew Will or not, the hookers on Aurora recognized him. Considered an okay guy, he had no trouble getting the girls to chat with him.

"Nah, she hasn't been out tonight."

"Reckon you can help me?" Will pulled out his card and spritzed it with cologne. "You recognize this scent?" After waving the card in the air a few times, Will handed it to the redhead.

She looked at Will and LaKeisha and laughed. "You 'spect me to remember some dude's cologne? You know how many dates I have in a day? A week?"

I know it's a longshot, but it's the best I've got in the Copycat killings."

The woman sniffed the card. "Nah, don't recognize it. Sorry."

"What's your name," LaKeisha asked.

"Pepper."

"I'm Detective LaKeisha Taylor, and this is Detective Will Cambrey," she said. "Keep the card. If you happen to smell this scent on some—"

"Some trick? Ya know, you's asking me to take some risks."

Will pulled out a twenty.

Pepper shook her head.

Will added another.

"Big risks."

"Ah, shit," Will handed her three more twenties. "I need the car make, color, and license plate."

"Right." Pepper smiled, revealing half-decayed front teeth.

Will turned to LaKeisha. "Let's talk to more girls."

CHAPTER 48

CATE REGRETTED DOING the press conference. From the moment she stepped down from the podium, she felt like the main attraction at a circus freak show. Her appearance at work as a serial killer's daughter created a feeding frenzy of predators who hid behind smiles and understanding looks.

When Cate had first come onto the floor after the news conference, a dead silence froze the moment she stepped off the elevator. Everyone glared at her as if her father's crimes had been her own. Several at the nurses' station whispered to each other and turned away.

Cate's first instinct was to get back on the elevator and go home. But instead, she held her head up high and walked straight to the nurses' lounge.

"Morning," Scott said, not looking her directly.

"So, I guess everyone is talking about my TV appearance."

"It's been mentioned," Scott replied. "No big deal."

"Right, no big deal. And that's why no one will look me in the eye?"

"It's not so much who your dad was. Some women are upset that you were promoting not only his but also the Copycat Killer's 'good side.'"

"I was doing it because the police—"

"Told you to appeal to his good side?" Scott shook his head. "And what, do you expect him to give you a call and take you to dinner?"

Cate grabbed her clipboard and stethoscope. "Fine. I don't care what any of you think. I'm helping to catch this guy while you all sit around gossiping like old ladies in a quilting circle." *So there!*

WILL'S APPEARANCE AT Harborview caught Cate off-guard, and she was not pleased.

"Thought you might like some lunch." Will held up a paper bag from Spud Fish and Chips.

"Will!" Cate said as she pulled him aside. "You know better than to just show up. What if Edward was here?"

"What? You two made up again?"

"No, but he could show up anytime."

"But he's not here now, right?"

Cate shook her head and gave Will a quick hug. "Whoa. You're wearing the same cologne that Edward wears."

Will pulled back from the hug. "Edward wears this scent?"

"Oh, c'mon, Will. You know he does. Is this supposed to be a practical joke? Not funny."

"How could I know Edward's cologne?"

"So, this is just a big coincidence?"

"I was at Nordstrom's yesterday, and the saleswoman recommended—"

"I'm free at two for lunch."

Will glanced at his phone. "You know what, I have to take a raincheck. Something just came up." He hugged Cate once again and with long swinging strides, walked to the elevator.

"Will, wait," Cate called just as the elevator doors opened.

As if lost in thought, Will stepped onto the elevator and glanced at Cate. He didn't seem to register she was calling his name.

THE ENTIRE DRIVE to the station, thoughts bombarded Will like bees on honeysuckle: *Edward wears the same cologne as the Copycat Killer. Edward picks up hookers on Aurora. Edward travels to Las Vegas often. Edward is the same height and weight as Jennifer Cannon's description.*

Once at his desk, Will called Jennifer and set up a time to visit her. As soon as he hung up, it dawned on him what was so familiar about that sketch— sure, he'd remembered that there was a slight resemblance to Edward—but as he pulled it out again, he couldn't believe what he'd missed. "Jesus Christ," he said louder than he meant to sound.

LaKeisha came right to his desk.

"Whatcha got, Will?"

"Nothing, just some follow-up work."

"Why aren't you telling me?"

"Telling you what?"

"The truth."

"What makes you say that?"

"Your right eye is twitching."

"Shit, Keisha."

"Go cry about it to someone else," Keisha said. "Spill it."

"Take a ride with me," Will said. "I'll explain it to you on the way."

"Where are we going?"

"We're meeting Jennifer Cannon at Cactus in Bellevue Square." Will grabbed his windbreaker.

"Maybe we can stop in Nordstrom? I want to get a bottle of that Tonka 25 for myself."

"COULD HE BE your attacker?" Will handed the photo of Edward to Jennifer.

Jennifer scooted her chair closer to the table. Filled with chatter, the waitresses and waiters scrambled to keep up. She grabbed a tortilla chip and dipped it in the salsa. "I don't know." She shrugged. "It was dark."

"Try to match his silhouette to this picture," LaKeisha added. "Does that help?"

"I mean, it could be him. But why would a guy who looks like this need to attack women?"

"The assault ain't—excuse me, ma'am—*isn't* about sex, it's about power and control," Will said.

"I showed him who had the power and control, right?" Jennifer straightened her back and lifted her shoulders.

"You sure did." LaKeisha patted Jennifer's hand that rested on the table. "You sure did."

CHAPTER 49

EDWARD TOOK EXIT 71 off I-84 on the outskirts of Boise, Idaho. Cars crowded the parking lot cars, and the Boise Stage Stop restaurant had a line out the door. Not wanting to wait, he pulled off the road to smoke a few hits. He slowed to a stop, opened his console, and grabbed his vape.

The spicy smoke tasted good as he inhaled the vapor. He took another puff and let the high soak into him. Perhaps he'd grab the French bread and cheese from the back? He closed his eyes and imagined the life he'd like to live. Free of The Darkness and all its demands. Free of the secrets that sat in the pit of his heart like a hot coal.

A light tapping on the window brought Edward out of his dreamlike state. On the passenger side, a young woman motioned for him to lower the window.

"Excuse me." Her voice was as light as daisy petals. "Are you heading toward Sedona?"

"Vegas."

He liked her soft blue eyes, her wispy blonde hair, and the way the breeze and the sun conspired to create a golden glow around her head.

Shit, the kid looks like an angel. Take her to the desert, and send her back to heaven, the self-serving entity said.

Edward blinked, and the vision of the halo disappeared.

"Would you mind if I hitched a ride?"

"You aren't a serial killer or anything like that?" Edward said, unveiling his charismatic smile.

The girl laughed.

"Why didn't Jeffrey Dahmer like clowns?" Edward kept a straight face.

"Why?"

"Because they tasted funny."

"Oh, God," the girl muttered.

"Don't worry," Edward said. "I'll keep the jokes to myself."

"Can I put my backpack in the backseat?"

"You need help with that?"

"Nah, I'm strong." She hefted the backpack in and climbed into the front seat.

Edward pulled onto Hwy 84 and hit the gas. As the setting sun bled into the sky, they headed south.

"I'm Edward." He did a quick study of her face. Her eyes were almost purple now, and her nose reminded him of Sophia, a Greek goddess of a woman he'd escorted to her grave a few years back.

"I'm Psyche." She pulled back her silky gold hair and tied it into a knot.

"Psyche? What kind of name is that?" Edward laughed. "Hippy parents, am I right?"

"No, I changed my name after my first vision quest."

The Darkness opened an eye and clucked, and Edward shot the entity a scowl.

"What's a vision quest?"

"A spiritual journey."

"Meaning?" Edward clicked on his headlights. The carcass of an animal filled the lane on the road ahead. He swerved to miss it. His mind bounced to the rabbit he'd killed when he was a kid. The thrill had been devastatingly pleasurable and had opened a door to research that had nothing to do with science.

"You learn how to be true to yourself. You know, be authentic. I woke out of my first visions a changed person. More in touch with my soul. I became a better person. I was finally free to just be me. A jaguar in the dream state told me to call myself Psyche, which means 'the soul.'"

Here we go with the woo-woo crap, the beast said. *We're smack in the middle of the desert. What could be more convenient than that? Hell, the mob buried plenty of bodies in the desert. She'd fit right in.*

Edward caught Psyche appraising him. "Whatcha thinking?" he said with a sly smile.

"Would you consider yourself a spiritual person?"

The Darkness choked back a laugh.

"If you mean, do I want to change, then yes."

"Well, I meant, do you wonder why you're here? What your soul's purpose is?"

"I don't know." Edward shrugged.

"Ah, come on. I'm a stranger. You can talk to me. Look at me. Jeans, boots, and a t-shirt—I was prom queen, for Christ's sake. Never wore pants. Never went out without makeup. Based everything on my outward appearance."

"We all wear masks in the world. I just sometimes feel burdened by mine."

"Edward, do you have a strong mind?"

"Yes. I'm an attorney."

"I mean, can you handle, you know, like hallucinogens?"

"I'd rather snort coke." Edward laughed, pulled out a cocaine bullet, and took a hit. He offered the container to Psyche, who shook her head.

"Do you want to take that mask off?"

"Sorry, I don't think that's an option?"

"Trust me. I can help." She touched Edward's arm. "Let's go on a vision quest under the moon." Excitement lined each word. "We can pull off and head into the desert. I have a tent, a flashlight and—"

"I have some food and a bottle of chilled champagne."

"Chilled champagne? Seriously?"

"You never know when you're going to need it."

Edward turned off Hwy 84 before Twin Falls and took a road leading away from the highway. As soon as he stopped the car, Psyche hopped out as if she had no fear, retrieved her pack, and headed into the night. "It's so clear. Check out the moon; it the color of butter."

Edward glanced at the wolf-eyed moon. The glow highlighted the sagebrush that seemed to crawl over the terrain like restless ghouls. He shrugged, grabbed the bread and cheese from the backseat, opened the trunk, and removed the champagne from the cooler.

Click-clack. Click-clack. Click-clack. Kill the angel. Kill her now, The Darkness urged.

Edward was in no mood for a confrontation with his goddamn albatross. He was focused on vision quests and how they'd changed Psyche. Could he change too? Rid himself of the monster eating his soul?

Click-clack. Click-clack.

Edward reached into his coat's inner pocket and pulled out his silver flask filled with Johnnie Blue. After taking a slug, he handed the container to Psyche, who held up her hand and waved him a "No."

Edward and Psyche walked until they found a ravine where they set up the tent. After unrolling a blanket across the ground, Psyche cleared a place for them to eat while Edward searched for kindling. He created a small teepee of twigs and brought an armful of broken branches.

Psyche sat next to the first flames that lifted into life when Edward squatted next to her. "So, how do we do this quest thing?"

"We drink some of this," Psyche said as she pulled a small glass container from her pack.

"What is it?"

"*Ayahuasca.* It's a brew from the Peruvian Jungle. I went with my brother."

Really? The Darkness said. *More hocus-pocus? I thought you hated that shit. Click-clack. She's on my nerves. Click-clack. Click-clack.*

"You're quite the traveler," Edward said. "And brave."

"More so fearless," she said and showed Edward a jaguar tattooed on her upper arm.

"Is it like Ecstasy?" Edward considered the detail of the jungle cat.

"Well, stronger. More intense. Psychedelic."

Edward added sticks, and the fire swelled as a dark cloud swallowed the moon. The flames grabbed for the crestfallen sky, and gray smoke curled in the breeze.

Click-clack. Click-clack. Click-clack. Click-clack.

Edward did not want to kill Psyche. She might have the key to set him free. Wanting to escape the creature's nonstop beak-snapping from pushing him over the edge, Edward turned to Psyche. "So, what happens when you drink it?"

The grinding of The Darkness' teeth drilled into Edward. The heaviness of his need to kill became too much to bear, and he clamped his fists and gasped for air.

"Everyone's quest is different, so I can't say what will happen to you."

Click-clack. Click-clack.

"Let's do it now," Edward muttered.

"I need to explain more to you—"

"Believe me, I can handle whatever happens," Edward said confidently.

"Your totem—spirit animal—might come to you. It will help you remove your mask."

The Darkness landed on Edward's shoulder and squawked.

Psyche took a sip and handed the vessel to him. "Be prepared to get sick at first—your body rids itself of toxins and—"

Edward slammed back the rest of the brew. "Jesus. That shit tastes terrible."

"We should sit. Get comfortable." Psyche added a branch to the fire.

In the distance, coyotes howled high, quavering cries. The moon, cloaked by thin black clouds, looked malignant and fierce.

And then it started.

Psyche crawled away from the fire, moaned, and vomited.

Edward's heart rate ramped. One moment, he was feverish, the next shivering. His hands and feet tingled, especially his palms. Minutes later, severe nausea hit. As if possessed by demons, his stomach felt cursed. The sensation, unlike any he'd ever experienced, moved through him in violent waves. He stumbled around to the back of the tent and vomited until his stomach felt shriveled. The whole desert seemed to spin. The sickness brought him to his knees, and he sweated like a field laborer too long in the sun.

Edward closed his eyes, and his mind opened a doorway into fractal shapes and colors. Reds spilled to oranges and purples to blues. Stars floated from the sky like illuminated snowflakes. He saw visions of himself stalking a woman into a dark cave. Behind him came thundering footsteps.

"Are you okay?" Psyche said as she rounded the tent.

As if thorns covered each word, Psyche's voice scraped at him.

"Of course, I am." Edward glanced up, but it wasn't Psyche who stood there. It was Patrick Derry.

A harsh jolt snapped through Edward, and he felt as if he were crumbling.

Scattering clouds unveiled the moon. Edward's mind jumbled like Boggle dice. He shook his head to break through a murky fog then focused on Derry.

"Edward." Derry spoke as if they were longtime friends. "What's that on your shoulder?"

"You can see it? It's The Darkness. It's going to make me kill her," Edward said, his voice trembling. "I don't want to."

"Sure, you don't," Patrick replied, not bothering to hide his sarcasm. "You never mean to kill them. Am I right, partner?"

"No, you know that's a lie. I'm not a killer. It's this creature," Edward shouted into the reckless night. "It makes me kill. It makes me suffer until I do."

"Whatever you say." The smirk on the Derry's face ignited a fever of blame in Edward. "You shouldn't speak about your totem with such distain," Derry warned. "Your soul chose that beast, and like all things, there was a trade—you bartered your body, which allowed it to work through you. In return, you were given power."

"What power?"

"The power to kill for the ultimate rush without remorse."

"I don't want it. How do I trade back?"

"Are you serious?" Derry laughed. "Sure, trade back. What the fuck do I care? But you'll miss the rush. You'll plead for The Darkness to return. You'll lose your power yet still be burdened by your addiction to it. In exchange, you'll find your authentic self *sans* mask."

The choice seemed simple—take the trade. But the clanging of confusion caused Edward to bring his hands to his head. "Stop! Stop," he cried into the desert's empty heart. When he uncovered his eyes, Psyche was next to him, in front of the fire, eyes fixed on the night sky.

"Isn't it beautiful?"

Edward felt a wave of sky splash through him. He looked up, hoping to see the beauty of the world. But a sinister undercurrent blinded him. Was Derry right? Had Edward chosen evil?

Impossible.

It was The Darkness that was evil. The Darkness that had pushed him to kill.

"I'm not evil," Edward muttered. A brutal fury tore from his heart as if a mother grizzly had ripped it out.

"Of course, you're not." Psyche took his hand. She still stared at the sky— her eyes as wide as heaven, but when Edward looked up, a plague of locust streamed across the moon.

"I wear a mask to hide it."

"Take it off. You can trust me."

The Darkness gagged in disgust. *Okay,* the beast said. *Let's give the lady what she's asking for. Tell her who you are."*

Edward hesitated. *What would it mean to tell her the truth? What's the worst that could happen? She would run off in fear?*

"I'm a serial killer. I kill for pleasure." He glanced at his strong hands that now looked blue.

Psyche continued to stare at the sky. "Look! Shooting stars."

"Don't you care? Aren't you afraid?"

"Afraid of what? I am a jaguar who kills prey with my jaws."

"Afraid that I will murder you."

Psyche pulled a knife from her boot. "Go ahead. Try."

The Darkness dug into Edward's shoulder and squawked louder. Then louder. A harsh jolt snapped through Edward, and hundreds of imaginary needles pierced tissue throughout his body. Pain screwed into his muscles each time they contracted. His hands ached with the need to kill. As did his mind. As did his heart. He felt like he was on fire. Every part of his body burned until the heat folded into itself and whooshed out of him like a swarm of bees. His mind cracked, and the perfume of violence intoxicated him.

Psyche stood there—her mouth moved, but Edward heard only the screeching of The Darkness.

Edward deserved to be free. He deserved to be included.

Tonight, his destiny lay in his hands. He could simply walk away. Remove the evil he'd worn like a hooded cloak for as far back as he could remember.

"You don't care that I get pleasure from killing women like you? That you could be next?"

Psyche glanced at him. "Yeah, right."

"I've killed over fifty women. The FBI is searching for me."

Psyche's eyes widened as if she finally understood the danger she was in and then seemed to turn to stone.

"I won't hurt you. I just want to be authentic. Like you." He felt torn. Why wasn't she moving? Why was that look of horror stretched across her face? He reached down to the broken branches and lifted a thick one. The urge to bash that look off her face engulfed him.

He listened for the click-clacking.

Nothing.

Edward threw the stick on the hot embers, and the flames ate the night. It was suddenly hot. Suddenly hard to breathe. He picked up another piece of wood and tossed it from one hand to the other. Snakes coiled up his legs. Rats scurried across his back. The heat beat down on him, and he broke into a sweat.

He took another minute to consider and finally understood what he had to do—prove he could be just like everyone else. Even though his need was as painful as a junkie's withdrawal, he would not kill. He no longer had to.

Edward stood. "Psyche, I am not evil. I don't have to kill. It's an evil entity that forces me . . . *I'm not evil. I am not evil. I am not evil.* He waited for The Darkness to spew its sarcastic remarks, but there was nothing. A profound relief set him free, and he relaxed. He considered the possibilities of a life well-lived.

Then.

As if The Darkness itself had swung the branch, Edward hit Psyche across her forehead. She crumpled to the desert floor. He beat her, then kicked her. Her cries, like a caught rabbit wailing in the night, became fainter—until she quit moaning. To be sure, he stomped her head. Then he fell to his knees.

He felt like he'd stepped into a prism. Colors bent, twisted together, then liquified. He raised his hands in ecstasy, lifted to the clouds, and hurled lightning bolts. Light fragmented into thousands of multicolored stars that spilled across the sky like glitter. The euphoria caused an uncontrollable shuddering, and thunder pounded the sky. The rapture sent exhilarating rushes through him.

When he came to, a fine mist dampened the air. He glanced at Psyche, who laid there dead, jaw opened in a silent scream, terror locked in her lifeless eyes. His hands matched his blood-soaked clothes. Everywhere he looked had been stained with the death of Psyche.

"What the fuck have I done?"

The sun had barely cracked the sky, his head pounded from the brew, and in the distance, he saw the entity flying toward the fading moon.

CHAPTER 50

"EDWARD, THIS IS Cate. I haven't heard from you. I know you are upset with me because I didn't tell you about the press conference, but the police insisted I keep it a secret. Please call me. I need to talk to you. Something has happened, and I'm . . ." She started to cry. "I just don't know how much longer I can cope."

Cate clicked off her cell and slumped into the couch. Ever since she'd been on the news, she'd felt uncomfortable at work. No one except Scott had mentioned it, but she could sense their disdain.

Only one nurse was kind to Cate. A new employee, Frances Lewis, had not been accepted into the clique of nurses who ran the floor. The loners, Cate and Frances, had a good rapport.

A knock on the door pulled Cate from her thoughts. She glanced at her phone. 9:30 p.m. The light from the moon sent a beam into her otherwise dark living room. She walked toward the front door and peeked through the peephole, but no one stood there.

"What?" she said, making her voice sound deeper and crazed. Will had told her that seeming unpredictable or that you might be more complicated than it's worth, kept predators from choosing you as a potential victim.

"It's Edward."

Cate unlocked the door and pulled it open.

Edward stood there, damp from the rain, a bouquet of wilted flowers in his hand.

"What a sorry sight I must be," Edward said. He held up the drooping daisies. "These were the only flowers they had."

"Oh, Edward!" Cate threw her arms around him. "I'm so sorry. I wasn't allowed—"

"Shhh, shhh," Edward said. "I don't want to fight anymore."

Cate pulled Edward into the house.

"I got your message and realized that I must come off as a real jerk," Edward said.

"No, not at all. I understand."

"Have they heard anything?"

"I don't know. I haven't been in touch with the police since the interview."

"Really. Hmm." Edward pulled off his windbreaker and headed into the living room while Cate grabbed a vase for the daisies.

"Let's go to Vegas. Leave tonight." Edward clicked on the floor lamp.

"It's almost ten."

"I don't care. I want you to be my wife. I can't wait any longer."

"I can't. I have to work tomorrow, and things have been—" Cate put the flowers on the coffee table and sat beside him. "Things at work suck."

"Jesus. I'm a thoughtless schmuck. You mentioned you were having trouble coping. Is it work?"

"Since the news conference, the other nurses avoid me—except for a new nurse, Frances. We have each other's back. Things feel uncontrollable. I worry that everyone might be suspicious and think I, being the Lace Ribbon Killer's daughter, have a proclivity toward murder and have—"

"Well, do you?"

"Edward!" Cate shot off the couch and faced him. "What the fudge does that mean?"

"Hey, just a joke," Edward said.

"Why are you so cruel?"

"I'm just trying to lighten the mood. You carry the world on your shoulders, Caitlyn." Edward pulled out his vape and offered it to her.

"What's that?"

"Let's get high."

"Since when do you do drugs?" Cate's mind flipped back a few slides to the day Will had told her Edward had done drugs with a prostitute.

"I have a new attitude. I'm now an authentic person." Edward offered a wink.

"I don't like it," Cate mumbled.

"You've never tried pot. How do you know you don't?"

"No, Edward. I don't like this being authentic thing. It means you haven't been telling me the truth."

"I took this time we had apart to do some work on myself. I went on what's called a vision quest. I heard about a place where they gave me spiritual tea, and it changed me. From that moment on, I am who I am."

We'll see about that, Cate thought. "Did you do drugs with that prostitute?"

Edward said nothing. He seemed lost in a haze.

"Well?"

"Yes, but let me explain."

Cate popped off the couch, crossed the room, and did a 180-degree turn. "You're a rat. A real sleaze."

"The girl was a friend I grew up with—the blonde cheerleader who went bad. She's got no one. Every so often, I pick her up, chat, get high, and bring her back. I give her some cash to help her out."

"And do you fuck her?"

"Jesus, Caitlyn, when did you start saying fuck?"

"I guess I'm being goddamn authentic too." She snapped her hands to her hips. "It doesn't matter if you did fuck her because I fucked Will." She grabbed her purse and headed upstairs. "How do you like your goddamn authenticity now? Huh?"

And *slam*.

She opened the door and *slammed* it again, locked it, reached into her purse for her phone, and called Will.

CHAPTER 51

WILL TURNED DOWN his TV and glanced at his buzzing phone. Cate. *Finally*. He'd been trying to reach her all day.

"Edward and I just had a fight, and I told him to fuck off," Cate whispered.

"Aw, geez, Cate—didn't you get my messages? I told you something's come up, and you need to stay away from the guy 'til I get some—"

"I don't want to hear your stories about Edward. I told you that, so just stop," Cate said firmly.

"I need to know you understand what I'm saying."

"Sure, yep, I heard you. He did some kind of quest thing and wants to be authentic with me."

"Cate. Are your doors locked?"

As if in her own cocoon, Cate continued. "Then he told me about a cheerleader prostitute he spends time with. I became furious and threw the fact that I slept with you in his face."

"Oh, God, Cate."

"I was being authentic." Cate stared out her window at the tree. Its branches, dim in the moonlight, rustled in the breeze. "Well, the truth is I wanted to hurt him."

"I'm on my way, you hear?" Will grabbed his shoes.

"You aren't listening to what I'm trying to say?" Cate snapped. "And if you come here, I will *never* forgive you."

Will sat back down. "Okay, what?" Will knew Cate, and if she didn't want to talk about something, you better just stop conversing right then.

"If I tell you something, will you promised not to get Edward in trouble?"

"Sure, what?"

"Promise?"

"Yeah. Okay."

"He does drugs. Pot and cocaine. He offered me a vape thingy, but I said no."

"I know he does. Remember? I mentioned it to you."

"Once, I found cocaine in his medicine cabinet, but he said it wasn't his. Ha!"

"Was it a little or a lot?"

"Just some in a pill container," Cate replied.

"*Was* there a little or a lot?"

"I don't know. I guess a little."

"Powder or rocks?"

"Why are you asking me all these questions?"

"I worry about you. The last thing I want is to hear you've tried coke. Maybe he deals, I mean, he does live quite the life. If he's got it, and you're there, you could get into some serious trouble. This whole thing is dangerous. I just wish you'd—"

"I don't want to talk about it anymore. With all your questions, it feels like you're going to get Edward in trouble. You promised, Will."

"One last thing, okay?" Will said.

"Not if it's about drugs."

"When's the last time he left town?"

"He just got back last night. He was on a self-awareness thing."

"Caitlyn?" Edward knocked lightly on her door.

"Whoops, he's outside my bedroom. I've got to go."

"Please let me in," Edward said softly from the other side of the door.

EDWARD'S HEAD FELT crammed in a pressure cooker ready to blow. His only choice now was to pretend as if Cate's betrayal with Will was forgivable, which it wasn't. To appear as if he were a changed man, he stuffed his fury until he had a chance to exact revenge.

He waited for The Darkness to chime in, but there was only a hard silence. Had he *really* left the beast in the desert in trade for his soul?

The bedroom door opened, and Cate let him in.

Framed prints of women painted by artist Itzchak Tarkay hung on the antique-white walls, the colors as vivid as irises and fuchsias.

"We should let go of the past. We were on-again, off-again when we fell backward." Edward moved around the room like a wound-up cartoon character. "Let's start over. No history. Drive to Vegas and get married. Commit to each other. Start our change with a new status." He took Caitlyn's hand. "You can move in with me. You know you love my home. And times are tough for you at work—you can quit if you want."

With ideas cluttering his mind, he tried to focus on Pipsqueak, whose head laid on a pillow and body stretched across the quilt. He tried to lasso his barrage of thoughts and forced himself to slow down.

Whew, he gasped. Satisfied he had said everything, he ambled to the bed, sat, and patted the mattress lightly. "Come sit next to me."

Caitlyn, hair down around her shoulders, wore a pair of pink pajamas with little red hearts printed on the fabric. "When would we go?"

"Now. You can jump in the Altima with your PJs and a pillow. You can even bring the stuffed orangutan your dad gave you."

"I'll need to pack. It takes two days to get there, right?"

Edward stood up again. "Mostly, I drive straight through, but I know a cute place to stay on the way. Let's go casual. Bring a pair of jeans and a couple of comfortable tops. We'll buy everything else there."

"I have to see if my neighbor will keep an eye on Pipsqueak and if Frances will cover my shifts. It's too late to call. We'll have to leave in the morning." Pipsqueak raised his head, looked around, and went back to sleep.

"Okay, I'll head home and pack."

"Oh gosh, I don't want you driving this late. What if you fall asleep on the way?"

"Okay, I'll be honest. I'm sniffing a pinch of cocaine—it will keep me awake." He didn't mention he'd be doing a sniff or two every fifteen minutes.

"I don't get it. Why do you do drugs when you have such a good life?"

"I don't use it to escape; I use it for fun. You know, you should try one little sniff. Trust me, you're going to like it."

"I thought it is white poison."

"Well, I suppose if you misuse it."

"I don't think I want to try it."

"One tiny bit. Just to see." Edward took a small container from his jacket pocket and a tiny spoon. With a scoop, he balanced cocaine into the bowl. "When you're ready, hold one nostril shut and sniff in hard with the other." He held the spoon under Caitlyn's nose.

Caitlyn gave a shrug and sniffed.

"What do you think?"

"I don't feel anything."

"Give it a sec."

"Wowzah!" she blurted. "It's like it's racing along my nerves like a bullet train. Holy Moly."

"I told you you'd like it."

"This is the best feeling!"

"Yep!" Edward scooped another spoonful of coke and snorted it. "Here, have one more."

"Really? Will I be up all night?" Caitlyn stared at the coke balanced on the spoon.

"Yeah, you'll be up but not because of the coke. You're coming home with me, and I'll make love to you until you pass out."

"Yum," Caitlyn said.

"Hey. What happened to the guy who accidentally mixed Rogaine in his cocaine?"

"I don't know." Caitlyn giggled.

"He's in the Guinness Book of World records for the world's longest nose hair."

Caitlyn shook her head. "Where do you get these jokes? Oh, that reminds me, I saw a news clip about the new world record in donut stacking. It was almost sixty inches tall and 3,100 donuts."

"I haven't heard this joke. Go ahead."

"No, seriously. It's true. It happened in Africa. We should try it." Caitlyn paced to the door and back. "Are there twenty-four-hour donut shops around?"

"Where are we going to get three thousand donuts?"

"Let's do one hundred then."

"How about we pick some up before we get into Vegas and do it there?"

"Yes," Caitlyn climbed on her bed, stood up, and bounced.

"Come here, my love."

Caitlyn slowed the bounce until she landed on the bed in a sitting position.

"'As if you were on fire from within. The moon lives in the lining of your skin.'"

"Neruda?" Caitlyn said with a smile.

"You can't get much better than him." With that, Edward took her hand and led her out the door. "Come on, Pipsqueak, you're coming too."

CHAPTER 52

WILL SAT FEET propped on his desk, hands behind his head. Debating his next move, his mind bounced from point to point. He'd spoken to Captain Thorten, who said to he should follow his hunches but to keep her informed.

He rechecked Cate's texts on his phone.

Cate: Going to Vegas to get married. Leaving tomorrow at noon.

Will: We need to talk first. Edward might be more dangerous than I thought.

There was no reply.

Will knew he couldn't tell Cate he liked Edward for the Copycat murders—*not until that snake-in-the-grass was behind bars. Cate tried to keep secrets, but Edward could squeeze the tar out of asphalt. Getting Cate to chitchat about the investigation wouldn't take much.* Will couldn't risk his case sliding backward. Edward must not get an inkling he's a suspect.

"Keisha." Will motioned to her as she chatted with Captain Thorten across the room.

Keisha ambled over to Will and sat in the chair across from his desk. "What can I do for you, buddy."

"I have a hunch that Cate Derry's fiancé might be a person of interest in the Copycat case."

"No kidding. Why?"

"Call it an instinct for now. I don't have proof yet. They're going to Vegas at noon. I'm going to follow them. Match the route he takes against the Copycat murders in Idaho, Oregon, Utah, and Nevada."

"Yeah, that's it?"

"I want you to go with me—Can you pack and be back here by ten?"

"Okay. Sure."

"I'll even take you to a show. Have you seen Cirque du Soleil? You'd love *O*."

"I've seen *Mystère*, that's all."

"Well, *O* might just be the best show you've ever did see."

"Ten o'clock then?" LaKeisha said.

Keisha smiled, but her eyes held something Will couldn't decipher.

CHAPTER 53

BY THE TIME Edward and Caitlyn hit Stanfield, Oregon, four hours had passed. Caitlyn's favorite pastime, so far, was singing with Edward. They started with oldies they both knew—Caitlyn kicked off with "Kryptonite," her first crush being Brad Arnold from 3 Doors Down. Edward's favorite was Britney Spears' "Oops . . . I Did It Again." They even sang the Beatles' tunes because everyone, no matter when they were born, knew, "I Want to Hold Your Hand" and "Help." Edward continued with corny jokes, and Caitlyn played the license plate game—she even saw Vermont and Florida.

"We'll drive another five hours, get a room in Twin Falls, and wake up early. We should be in Vegas by tomorrow night."

When they were an hour from Twin Falls, Edward said, "I should have brought a tent and some camping gear."

Camping? Out here? In the desert? What about snakes and scorpions? And God forbid, the Copycat Killer. Caitlyn rubbed the back of her neck. "Speak for yourself, Mr. Outdoors."

"What, you wouldn't camp with me?"

"There are too many variables. I'd feel vulnerable." Caitlyn glanced at the desert that stretched as far as she could see.

"You know I'd never let anything hurt you." Edward glanced at her with a smile.

"But snakes and the Copycat—"

"Don't worry about the Copycat, ever." Edward patted her leg.

"Why's that?"

"Because you're the daughter of a serial killer. All you'd have to do is tell him that."

Caitlyn rolled her eyes. "That's not going to work, and you know it."

"Whatever. I doubt the Copycat would stalk people in the desert, anyway."

"That's reassuring."

"Caitlyn, I'd kill the bastard before I'd let him come close to you."

"Now *that* makes me feel safe." Caitlyn took Edward's hand.

The night draped the sky like a silk curtain and showcased the face of the moon.

CHAPTER 54

"KEISHA," WILL TAPPED Keisha's shoulder.

Keisha, who had laid back and slept in the passenger seat of the Prius rental, stirred. "Huh?" She wiped her mouth and opened her eyes.

"It's six. You've got the morning shift."

"Shit, already?" Keisha stretched her arms.

"A fella can only stare at a vehicle in a parking lot for so long."

Keisha glanced in the backseat. "Any of those chips left?"

"Hold on. Hold on." Will pointed at Edward's Altima across the street. "They're getting in the car."

"We don't have time to switch. Can you keep driving?" Keisha asked.

"Don't have much choice. And they're off." Will started the ignition, waited for the Altima to get farther down the road, and pulled away from the curb.

Six hours in, Edward and Cate pulled into Chester's Chicken to Go south of Crystal Springs, Nevada. Will and Keisha watched as the two climbed out of their car and headed into Chester's. Ten minutes later, they came out with several large bags and drinks.

"Damn," Will said, his stomach growling. "I'm fixin' for some chicken."

"Count me in," Keisha replied.

Once in Chester's, Will flashed his badge to the counter server and showed him the photo of Edward. "Did you see this guy who was in here about ten minutes ago?"

"Yeah, you just missed him."

"He ever come here before today—I mean that you can remember?"

"Yes, sir," the kid answered. "He stops here pretty often."

"Is he always alone?"

"Yes, sir. He do something wrong?"

"No. This is just routine. Have you ever seen him do, say, or act unusual?"

"Well, now that you mention it. He's the only person who tips the counter people. Nice guy, huh?"

"Yeah, a real star," Will replied.

"Are you gonna order, sir?"

"Give us two combos," Keisha said. She glanced at the menu. "And a couple of your homemade donuts."

"Sorry, ma'am, that guy you been asking about bought them all. His lady friend was talking about stacking them."

"Stacking them?" Keisha said.

The kid shrugged, grabbed the combos, and rang the food up.

Back in the car. Keisha zipped onto Hwy 93, and twenty minutes later, they saw Edward's Altima about a quarter-mile ahead. The rest of the trip was uneventful. As soon as they hit Vegas, they watched Edward pull up to the valets in front of the Venetian hotel.

CHAPTER 55

CAITLYN WALKED INTO their penthouse suite and stopped in her tracks. The floor to ceiling windows provided a spectacular view of the strip and farther. "Holy Jeez," she said.

The formal living area was elegant with a cream-colored couch and two matching wing chairs. Behind the couch and sharing the salmon, blue, and gray oriental rug was the dining area. A vase with fresh flowers sat in every room. "And, oh my gosh, a piano! A sunken tub with a jacuzzi. A steam room. Edward, come see the fireplace in the master bedroom."

"Gorgeous. Exactly what you deserve. I'm going to check out that bathroom. Do you want to use it first?"

"Nah, I should give Frances a call and check on Pipsqueak." Caitlyn grabbed her phone and clicked it on. She saw six text messages—all from Will. She opened the first:

Will: We need to talk first. Edward might be more dangerous than I thought.

Just then, Edward came from behind and grabbed Caitlyn in his arms and threw her on the bed. He climbed up next to her, stood on the mattress, and jumped up in the air.

Caitlyn burst into laughter. Like a gleeful child, she watched the silly faces Edward made every time he bounced up and down. She set her cell on the nightstand, stood up—barely balancing—and joined Edward until they both, exhausted and giggly, made their final landing.

"Sometimes, you surprise the heck out of me," Caitlyn wrapped her arms around Edward.

"How so?"

"I never dreamed I see the day that Edward 'The Cool' Olson would let go and play like a kid."

"When did I play like a kid?"

"Just then. Jumping on the bed in a swanky hotel."

"I'll have you know that was quite adult-like," Edward said, feigning seriousness. "*This* is acting like a child." With that, he turned on his side and tickled Caitlyn.

Caitlyn burst into laughter until tears formed in her eyes. "Stop! Tickling is torture. They say that now." She paddled her hands up and down like a cartoon character mock fighting.

Edward grabbed her wrists. "Do you prefer this little bitch?" And he pinned her down.

"Well, that's a tough choice. I like it when you're childlike."

"But?"

"I like you AGGRESSIVE, as well."

"*Moi? Agressif?*"

"*Oui. Tu.*"

AT THAT MOMENT, Edward's other thoughts screeched to a stop. *Do you hear that?* He called to The Darkness. *She likes that I'm aggressive.* He waited for a sarcastic reply, but there was nothing but the silence of being on his own. Which he preferred. Right?

"Caitlyn," Edward said softly. "What if I told you I was more aggressive than you could imagine? Would you like me still?"

"You know I love you. It's unconditional. Like my love for my dad."

"What if I was more like your dad than you thought?"

Caitlyn grabbed a pillow and hit Edward over the head. "You're such a nut! Make love to me right now, Mr. Aggressive, and I'll show you exactly how I feel."

"But I—"

Before he could finish his sentence, Caitlyn's lips had found his.

It was moments like this that Edward felt a pull, but he didn't know how to define it. More and more, Caitlyn seemed drawn to his edge, and he liked it. He liked it a lot. And he felt free. Free of The Darkness that had controlled him. Free of the rage that had sucked on him like a starving tick. Free of the need to destroy a life.

That is until 3:15 that morning.

Edward's inner rage spew him out of a nightmare. He needed release, and he needed it now. He headed to the bathroom and peered into the mirror. There, looking straight back at him, was his reflection, his gaze as sharp as the Reaper's scythe. He walked over to the double-doors that led to the hallway. Then to the living room. The dining room. The powder room. The piano. Back to the bathroom. He paced the circuit again. And again. With each completed round, the anger seared deeper into him.

He held his forehead between his hands and waited for The Darkness to show up and pressure him about a kill, but there was nothing. Even though the demon hadn't shown its face, Edward suspected that the beast watched from the shadowy edge of death, and it suffered too. No killing; no high. He took a couple of swigs of scotch. A line of coke. And several hits off his vape. He threw on a t-shirt, stepped into a pair of dark jeans, headed back into the bathroom, and peered in the mirror.

I am not evil. I don't have to kill. The death of Psyche was an accident. It was the drug, not me.

He sat in the living room and looked out to the strip. There, in the UV lamps high outside the Venetian, grasshoppers swarmed like an apocalyptic prophecy. Watching the insects dive for the light, he considered his options, finally deciding his best move was to open another bottle of Johnny Blue, snort a few more lines and get stoned.

By five-thirty, Edward was drunk and strung out. He walked to the piano, sat down, and barely brushed the keys with his fingers as he played "Mariage d'Amour."

"Edward?" Cate walked into the living room. "I didn't know you played." She stood behind him with her hand on his shoulder. "I love this music."

"This is our wedding day, my love."

"It's not even six."

"The chapel opens at nine. Get ready."

"I don't have a dress."

"We'll rent it at the chapel."

"What if they don't have anything I like?"

"They will."

"How do you know? Have you done this before?"

"Of course not." Edward stood and took Caitlyn into his arms. "Nervous?"

"I guess so."

"Do you love me?"

"Yes."

"And you know I love you?"

"Yes."

"Then?"

"I'll take a shower."

CHAPTER 56

CATE DECIDED TO bathe in the sunken tub. She drizzled a few drops of lavender oil in the steamy bath, turned on the jacuzzi, and stepped in. The water, now steamy, felt divine as she submerged to her neck. She took a deep breath and let out a sigh.

She hadn't had a chance to take everything in—from Edward's suggestion to get married until this very moment—and it felt good to be alone with her thoughts. She scooted down, so her head slipped underwater. Everything quieted, and her mind floated on a memory's breeze.

Is this what death felt like?

Cate's relationship with death was somewhat off-center. She firmly believed in an afterlife in another world. After they killed her father, he would visit her late at night. He'd sit on her bed and tell her stories about death. He said it was a "happy" place, and that he'd done all those women a favor by removing them from life's worries.

"How come you didn't kill me?" she had asked.

"Because some people have a purpose and need to stay alive."

"What's my purpose, Daddy?"

"Hey, how'd it go with that earthworm report today?"

"Okay. I brought my earthworm to school and showed it when I read my report," she answered.

"And?"

"After school, I put it on the ground and stepped on it."

"Really? Why?"

As if lost in thought, Cate was quiet for a minute. "I didn't want it to have to deal with life's worries. Right, Daddy?"

"Right, Sugar Plum."

Cate flashed back into now, came up from the water, and drew in a large breath. She had time to consider Will's texts. *What the heck could Will's messages be referring to*? Yes, Edward was dangerous and aggressive—but "get away from him as soon as possible?" Fiddlesticks!

CAITLYN HAD CLICKED on the jacuzzi jets and had her eyes closed.

"Hey, babe." Edward placed his hand on her Caitlyn's shoulder, and she opened her eyes. He took a moment to consider the vagueness that deepened the hue of her irises into a smoky blue. Something was eating at her. "What's up?"

"Nothing, just thinking."

"Anything special?"

"We haven't built our donut stack." Caitlyn turned on the hot water.

"We only have about thirty."

"Then we need seventy more. I want to stack a hundred."

"There *are* a bunch of donut shops on the strip."

"Let's build it! Now."

"Now?"

Caitlyn nodded her head. "Pretty please."

"I'm marrying an eccentric." Edward laughed. "I'll stop by my office and pick up some files while I'm out," he lied.

The sparkle had returned to Caitlyn's eyes, and she seemed enthusiastic.

"Good. I'll leave now." Edward kissed Caitlyn's cheek. "You get dressed and be ready when I get back."

"Sure thing," Cate said. She gave Edward a flirtatious wave. "See you soon, handsome."

Edward grabbed his wallet and headed out the door.

CAITLYN CLIMBED OUT of the tub, dried off, put on the plush Venetian robe, and wrapped a towel around her head like a turban. Sitting on the edge of the jacuzzi, she picked up her phone and returned to Will's messages. He sounded even more adamant. She didn't like his behavior. He was trying to ruin her wedding day. He was a cop who was nosing around in her business. As if she had just bungee jumped, her stomach dropped, and emptiness consumed her. Edward was getting the attention of the Seattle Police. What he may have done wasn't as important as the attention he was drawing to himself . . . and consequently, her. Marrying Edward would create one of life's worries. She knew that now.

CHAPTER 57

"HONEY, I'M HOME." Edward closed the suite doors behind him and chuckled. He'd never dreamed he'd say those words—okay, he *had* said those words occasionally. Like when he stood over a sleeping woman after he'd broken into her home. He'd shake her shoulder, say the words, and rip her from her dreams into a nightmare. But to a woman he was about to marry? If only his father-in-law-to-be were still alive. He imagined Patrick Derry walking Caitlyn down the aisle.

He reveled in his change of fortune. After Psyche, he'd made a courageous choice to leave his cohort, his dark companion, his Darkness, in the desert. At first, riddled with anxiety, he worried that the obtrusive creature would return to enslave him once again. But all had been quiet.

He placed the bags of donuts on the bar. "It's your lucky day. I got seventy plus an extra for me to put on top." He grabbed a donut and bit into it. "I mean sixty-nine plus one."

The suite was quiet. Caitlyn was probably still in the tub, head underwater, daydreaming about getting married. He'd asked her to be ready. One thing that bothered him was her stubborn streak. She'd have to learn that he ran the show.

"Caitlyn?"

He wandered into the bathroom. The tub was empty.

"Caitlyn?"

Once in the master bedroom, he stopped in his tracks. Caitlyn's side of the walk-in closet was empty, her purse and jewelry were no longer on the dresser, and her overnight case was gone.

What the fuck?

He called Caitlyn immediately. Her outgoing message had changed from, "This is Cate. Please leave a message," to "I'm sorry, I'll be unreachable for the next few days. Leave a note. I'll call you when I return."

An avalanche of rage rumbled through him and left an icy demeanor in its wake. *It's times like this . . .* he thought as he clenched and unclenched his fists.

His teeth locked together until his jaw ached. The pounding in his ears created a fog that left him unattached to himself, disoriented, and broken.

Unfocused and seeing only red, Edward stumbled into the bathroom. He splashed water on his face to combat the dizziness; the urge to vomit overwhelmed him, but the seething anger and desire for vengeance pushed him to a level he thought no longer existed.

Adrenaline rushed through him.

"Fuck! Fuck! Fuck!" he yelled.

He staggered into the living room, grabbed the Tiffany standing lamp, and smashed the glass shade against the wall. Like the scattering of multicolored birds, broken pieces flew everywhere. Using the lamp's stand as a bat, he struck the chandelier, banged all the bottles off the bar, hit the refrigerator and broke a TV screen.

And then, as if the storm had passed, he felt nothing.

AFTER FOUR HOURS of driving home, Edward stopped for a restroom break. He did a gas fill-up at the Shell in Ely and was back on the road. With each mile, the fury coiled more until his brain felt tight and ready to spring. The urge to kill continued to build, but he tried to disavow it.

It's not me, he thought. *I am a puppet, and The Darkness pulls strings from some unseen shadow. I will drive to Seattle and set things straight with Caitlyn once and for all. But what, exactly, did setting her straight entail?*

In the distance, he saw movement on the side of the road. As he came closer, a woman in cut-off jeans, a red plaid shirt, cowboy boots, and a hat pulled low on her brow, stuck her thumb out as he approached.

A cowgirl. I'd sure like to see that filly kick. He imagined her face turning blue as her life force dulled her bloodshot eyes. The fantasy slammed him back. *Goddamn it.* One moment he was free from the burden, the next, his thoughts circled like bulimic buzzards ready to binge. The desire to stop, pick up the girl, and take her for a *real* ride ping-ponged through him.

I'll just drive right on by. "I will not stop. I am good. I will not stop. I am not evil," he mumbled.

He drove past her and sighed with relief. Or was that a fantasy too? Because when he snapped out of his thoughts, he was pulled over and flirting with the girl. She climbed in the car and flashed a smile, but all he could think of was Caitlyn. *The bitch didn't stay around to talk things over. The bitch was selfish. Out of control.* Edward felt on edge. Confused. *I'll just give this cowgirl a ride to where she's heading. I'm a good person.* And even though The Darkness refused to show itself—he glanced into the rearview mirror, just to be sure—he sensed that the beast was along for the ride. It had to be.

"Blah, blah, blah, blah, blah," the carefree woman jabbered on and on. Something about tarot cards. Something about fate. "Would you like a reading?"

"Huh?"

"I'll read your cards." She lifted a leather pouch out of her bag.

Oh, Christ, Edward thought. Just what he needed—a long ride in the desert with a cowgirl psychic.

"All you have to do is pick a card, and I can tell you what's going on with you." She fanned the deck for Edward to choose.

"No, thanks." Edward's left foot tapped, his mouth felt parched, and adrenaline flooded through him. "I'm not big on hocus-pocus crap."

"C'mon. It's not fortune-telling. It will give you information about yourself."

"I know everything I need to know."

"Look, check this out. This one's for you." The cowgirl selected a card and flipped it over. Above the word, "Death," was a black and white sketch of a hideous creature. Its bird-shaped head resembled The Darkness, and its skeletal body covered with straggly feathers showed no semblance to anything good. The background was blackened by small spear-like lines that slanted like windblown rain. At the top, in a white squiggly circle, was the Roman numeral XIII.

"Well, *that* doesn't seem like a good omen," Edward said, glancing into the rearview mirror. "Pick another." His voice sounded empty and flat.

"Death isn't a bad card. It can mean a big change is on the horizon—"

"Pick another," Edward repeated.

"Let's take the next turnoff, and I'll give you a full reading."

Edward turned onto a barren side road and stopped near a group of cacti that surrounded a mound. "Let's go there." He pointed toward the hill.

I will not hurt this woman. I made a trade. I have a soul now.

Once they reached the top of the small rocks, they found a spot clear of the sharp, pointed carpet of headed barrel cacti. The woman grabbed a sweater from her bag, laid it on the dusty ground, and set her tarot deck on top.

"So, tell me about the Death card. Does it mean someone is going to die?" *How ironic if it did.* Edward chuckled.

"Well, it could mean that, but it usually means transition. Something big will cause the death of the old and the birth of the new."

Edward had a snippet of a fantasy. He'd catch up with Catelyn and then he'd . . . As if a thunderbolt of frustration had hit him, an electric burn shot through him. His pulse quickened, and his heartbeat thumped. The pain felt like a screw boring into his brain. He couldn't stand the sensation. His mind suddenly seemed wrung dry.

"Hey, are you praying?"

God, she's an idiot. Edward opened his eyes. He didn't like this girl and her voodoo cards. He scanned the desert floor for something to shut her up with. He felt dizzy. What was he doing? What was his plan? As if his mind suddenly fractured, his thoughts fragmented then crumbled. An irregular, cranking sound filled his ears. He grabbed them with both hands and shook his head vehemently. What was this plan? Why was he here? Who was this girl?

The girl's face drained of all color. She shifted to a squat, scooped her cards into a pile, straightened them, and returned them to their pouch.

Edward saw the cards and remembered why they had stopped. "Hey, hey, hey." He tried to speak over the noise in his head. "What about my reading?"

"You don't seem very interested. Anyway, I need to get back on the road."

The shakiness in the girl's voice turned a switch on in Edward's mind. The scent of fear was an elixir—a drug more potent than mainlining meth.

"Yes. I'm interested. Let me pull one card then."

The girl pulled the deck out of the pouch and fanned the cards, which shook slightly in her trembling hands.

Edward paused, picked a card near the end of the deck, and handed it to the girl. She flipped it over to reveal a card with the words, "The Tower," written across the bottom. In a jagged white circle at the top, the number XVI. The image showed bolts of lightning striking an evergreen tree. The treetop had been broken and roared with fire. The lower portion of the tree looked ready to topple. Figures of people, both strong and weak, rich and poor, fell from the branches.

"Well?" Edward took the card back. "Shit, this isn't the most uplifting tarot deck I've ever seen."

"Change never looks comfortable until we look back. Then we can say whether it was a good thing or not."

"Meaning?"

"I see . . ." As if uncertain about relaying the interpretation, the girl hesitated. "A collapse of what you know. Chaos that leads to a breakthrough. Looks like you're journeying through a dark night of the soul."

"What the fuck is that?"

"Things might seem desperate, but it will pass. In the end, you'll have a deeper insight into yourself."

"I don't like it." Edward felt the insidiousness of self-doubt creep up his spine. "This is bullshit." His anger—a potent brew of hurt, frustration, and fear had churned in him from as early as he could remember and balled him like a clump of heavy metal in his heart. It was hard to breathe, harder to think. He pushed himself to his feet and grabbed for the girl.

The girl, still squatting, rolled forward, causing Edward to trip over her. She sprung to her feet, whipped around, and smashed his groin with her heavy cowgirl boot. The girl howled like a wild banshee and kicked him several times.

Edward finally stumbled. The girl gave him a swift push causing him to tumble back down the mound. He smacked into a patch of piercing cacti. Excruciating pain from the spines as they punctured his back overwhelmed him. The girl's constant kicking enraged him. He screamed as he extracted himself. "I'm going to kill you, bitch."

The fist-sized rock she threw smacked Edward on his forehead as he pushed himself up, and the girl took off. As if she were a runner going for the gold, she dashed toward the highway.

Weakened from the harsh kicks, Edward fell to his knees. His back hurt like hell from the punctures, and his genitals ached to his core. Trying to chase the pain away, he pulled out a cocaine bullet from his pocket and snorted two hits of coke, then two more. He glanced down the sandy, dirt road. The girl was gone. He wanted to catch her, but his legs refused to rev. *If she's on the main road, I'll find her.*

Regardless, he knew he better haul ass out of there before the police showed. He trudged to his car, downed three gulps of scotch, sped to the highway, and barreled toward Boise.

CHAPTER 58

WILL AND KEISHA were about twenty miles north of Ely when they saw a dirt road with crime scene tape wrapped around two large cacti and across its entrance. As they pulled to the side, Will saw the flash of police lights farther up the hard-packed, unpaved road. They climbed out of the car and approached the two officers who chatted near the yellow tape.

Both Keisha and Will pulled out their IDs and introduced themselves.

"So, what do we have going on here?" Keisha asked.

"It's under control," the burly, redheaded officer replied coolly.

Just great. We've got one of those officers who doesn't like to share information, Will thought. "We're out here investigating a serial killer known to drive this highway. You got anything for us on that?"

The redheaded officer shrugged, but the other said, "Yeah, a girl was assaulted but escaped. They've taken her to the hospital."

"How bad is she hurt?" Keisha asked

She's pretty scraped up, but she's okay."

"Which hospital?" Keisha pulled her cell phone out.

"William Bee Ririe in Ely."

"Got it." She turned toward Will, who had wandered up the uneven road and was talking to the officers. "Will," she yelled and waved.

"It's Edward," he called out as he ran down the road, almost falling twice. "*What?*"

"I knew it." Will gasped as he spoke. "The girl knew his name, described *his* car, *his* face, *his* hair," he muttered. "And they found a lace ribbon."

"Jesus, Will, I just can't believe it. He's such an all-American guy."

"*Really?* Edward?" Will replied.

Keisha shrugged. "So was Bundy."

At that moment, everything came to a thundering stop. All Will could think of, all he could worry about, was Cate. Where had she been while all this was happening? Was she at the Venetian sitting at the pool? Shopping in Caesar's Palace? At the craps table bringing somebody luck? Or, dear God! Murdered?

He grabbed his cell phone from his back pocket and dialed her number.

"I'm sorry, I'll be unreachable for the next few days. Leave a message. I'll call you when I return."

"Cate, stay away from Edward. If you see or hear from him, call me ASAP." Will hung up. What if she was still at the hotel? Could Edward have left her there, dead?

CHAPTER 59

EDWARD HAD ZIPPED past Boise and was closing in on Baker City, Oregon. He was tired, and the damn punctures in his back hurt. He'd driven nonstop since the girl assaulted him. He glanced at the clock. *Jesus, it had been almost eight hours.* As much as he wanted to rest a few hours, he kept going, snorting coke to stay alert and awake. He was on a roll and wanted to get to Seattle.

How had he gotten so sloppy with the cowgirl? When he tried to review the scenario in his mind, it presented more like a dream rather than an actual event. He hadn't planned to hurt her. He wasn't like that anymore . . .

Right?

What would he have done if he hadn't been so disoriented as he sat, surrounded by cacti, hearing his fate from a cowgirl with a deck of cards who talked about death and chaos? If he'd gotten the girl under his control, then what? He wouldn't have hurt her.

Or was he lying to himself?

Was his self-centered dark companion watching from the shadows? Pushing Edward's mind with whispers that rode the heated breeze? Enticing him to kill? Yes. That had to be it. Because Edward was a good person haunted by a demon who still, even when no longer at his side, wanted him to kill.

Edward glanced at his reflection in the rearview mirror. For a nanosecond, he thought he saw the creature sitting on his shoulder. He closed his eyes then looked again. The Darkness was gone.

And what the hell would he do when he finally caught up with Caitlyn? If she hadn't been Patrick Derry's daughter, he would have taken her life on day one, visited her body along the Green River, and not have dealt with all the goddamn emotional crap.

How could she have betrayed him in such a cruel way?

A sharp pain clamped in his chest. His throat felt tight, and his breathing labored. How. Could. She. Have. Done. This. To. Him? Had she taken pleasure in setting him up and then ripping everything away? He was sure that the bitch had.

He'd tear her fucking heart out.

CHAPTER 60

CATE WOKE UP from her nap, still exhausted. It was hard to believe that just that morning, she'd skipped out on Edward, grabbed a taxi, and headed for the airport. The plane trip from Vegas had been hectic, the cab ride home, slow. She still had a few days off but called the hospital to look for extra shifts to fill in the time. She offered to pull a double for Frances, whose kid was sick, which left Cate scheduled for that night and the morning shift.

Even though Cate and Frances had coffee together a few times a week, when it came down to it, their relationship was one-sided. Frances confided in Cate about her ex-boyfriend, her twelve-step program for overeaters, and her fears of being alone. Cate would small talk, never discussing anything behind the murky veil that shrouded her soul.

Not only had her mother taught her not to trust anyone, but her father also echoed those sentiments often. "Everyone wears a mask," he'd told her. "And when you least expect it, they will turn on you. Even your mother."

Which was true. Her mother had turned on Cate when Maddie died. Cate was like a lovely ladybug. Her mother, a Venus flytrap, had imprisoned Cate's spirit from birth.

When Maddie had wanted to play a mermaid, Cate had helped by holding her under the water. At first, Maddie wiggled like a dancing fish, then she quieted. Maddie's ability to stay underwater fascinated Cate. Even though she suspected this was wrong, okay, knew it was wrong, she had continued to hold her sister under—until she'd heard her mother clumping up the stairs.

Sure, Cate had revealed personal facts to Edward. But only pieces. She lied by omission, a phrase that bothered Cate. She didn't consider the partial truth a lie. Whoever made up that rule was mistaken. A lot of rules were mistakes.

Speaking of mistakes, she had known she couldn't marry Edward. And now she understood why. Cheeses! How had she let herself end up in Vegas? Because it was hard for her to say no to Edward . . . just like it had been with her father. Strength and darkness surrounded both men. Cate had recognized it in her father and now felt it in her fiancé.

Sometimes, when she was alone, she sensed Edward in the room—somehow watching, somehow peering into her thoughts. She was like a spring flower and Edward, the sun. His charisma, his nonjudgmental thinking, his protectiveness, and his edginess had caused her to bloom. But lately, he'd inched too close to the Caitlyn behind the mask. Trying to cast light on her shadow side. An impossible situation. Edward was too nosy. Too controlling. Too stubborn. Throw in Edward's authenticity kick. It was a recipe for disaster.

Cate peered into the mirror and changed her mind. Instead of the barely pink lipstick she'd already applied, today would be red, the color of strength and determination. A color that captured her mood.

Would Edward come looking for her? She counted on him going home and brooding over his loss of control, which gave her time to consider her plan.

Cate put on her new scrubs—the top decorated with colorful, small butterflies, and the pants a matching green. She twisted her hair into a makeshift bun and secured it with a hair stick. On her way to work, she'd stop at CVS and purchased red lipstick.

With that, Cate grabbed a snack and her keys.

She was ready to face the day.

CHAPTER 61

AFTER TALKING WITH the assault victim at the hospital and several officers from Ely, LaKeisha and Will planned to stop at gas stations and restaurants as they headed north on Hwy 93 toward Boise. Several employees had recognized Edward's picture and called him a "sort-of" regular. A cash-paying customer. They'd remembered because when Edward seemed happy, he'd leave a 25-percent tip.

Will shot one question after the next, keeping notes of locations, witnesses' names, and dates and times when he could.

Had the guy stopped for a snack, the restroom, or to get more gas?

Was he alone?

Did he stop there today?

What was his demeanor?

Could they see today's video from the security cameras?

They got a hit at their first stop—the gas station in Ely. The girl behind the counter remembered Edward from that morning because he'd seemed lost, disoriented, and distracted.

"Can we take a look at your security video?"

"Gotta ask the boss." The girl blew a small bubble with her gum until it snapped. She punched the number into her cell phone and gave a nod when her boss picked up.

Will took the phone and explained the situation.

The boss, who introduced himself, said he only lived a few miles away, and he'd be at the station in twenty. After clearly seeing Edward enter and leave the store, with the date and time stamp on the video, Will asked the manager if he could keep the video. Will wrote a makeshift receipt, and he and Keisha left with their evidence. They recognized that they were stepping on the toes of the local investigators, but they couldn't risk losing this vital information.

Back in the car again, Will and Keisha high-fived. Now they could show that Edward had been at that gas station less than an hour before the assault. Will's intuition had spotlighted Edward from the moment they'd met, and now he knew he'd been right.

Although thrilled about the video evidence, Will's focus centered on Cate. He tried her phone again, but no answer.

"Why don't you try calling the hospital where she works," Keisha said. She blew a bubble with the gum she'd bought at the gas station. Then, she blew another bubble inside the first.

Will popped the bubbles with his finger and pink, thin strings covered Keisha's nose and mouth like a web. "See, that's what I like about you," he said. He tapped his finger on his temple and nodded. "Smart."

"You're just not thinking straight. Call her now."

As Keisha pulled into a small diner, Will was already on hold with the nurses' station.

Thank God, Will thought, relieved that he'd found Cate.

"What?" Cate's voice, carrying an edge of irritation, came on the line. "This better be a real emergency, Will."

"I need you to stay away from Edward—"

"Really, Will? *This* is your emergency? You've already left me plenty of warnings. I don't have time for—"

"It's serious. He's more dangerous than I thought. He's brutal, Cate."

A sudden silence.

"He cannot know we're onto him." Will hoped to win Cate's confidence.

Silence still.

"I won't be back in Seattle until tomorrow. Go to my place when you get off and stay there." Will's voice softened. "Are you okay?"

"Yes . . . okay. I work a double so—"

"Have someone walk you to your car and then go to my house."

"What has he done?"

"We'll talk when I see you."

"*No!* Tell me now, or I'll go home after work."

Will hesitated. "You can't tell this to Edward, Cate. This is crucial. Lives depend on it."

"In the vault, Will."

"I need more than the vault.

"Okay. Okay. So what?"

"We can prove he's the Copycat Killer."

CHAPTER 62

BY THE TIME Edward got to Caitlyn's, he was so revved up on the coke that the fourteen-plus hours had flown by. He drove into Seattle close to four a.m., headed straight to Caitlyn's condo, parked outside the complex, and climbed the fence. The place was dark. He grabbed Caitlyn's key she hid in a fake rock near the back door.

The door to the kitchen creaked when he came in. Edward hesitated, waiting for Pipsqueak to bark, but the dog was quiet. Shit. Even if a marching band accompanied him, he knew the dog would sleep through it.

In the alcove, only a nightlight burned. Its blue, dim light shape-shifted ordinary silhouettes into a nightmare menagerie. The plant on the small table looked like a monstrous spider, the overhead fixture hung like a fat bat. Even the vacuum cleaner, pushed to the side, resembled a hunchbacked old woman casting a spell.

In the distance, he heard the jingling of bells that got louder with each breath he took until the noise vibrated like a slammed gong. His mind spun in reverse. His rage twisted into the image of Caitlyn, his ultimate trophy. The urge to destroy her, overwhelming. What about his allegiance to Patrick Derry? What about rescuing his own soul?

He shook his head to stop the revolving thoughts, and the wavelike shrill from the gonging. As he stepped into Caitlyn's bedroom, a wave of violence burst through him.

"Honey, I'm home," he roared. He flicked on the bedroom light ready to pounce, but an unslept-in bed was all he found. Fuse lit, Edward searched her office, the living room, and everywhere else.

His savage need propelled him back to his car. Once there, he snorted—well, he really wasn't sure how many hits of cocaine he did—enough coke to put him on top of the world. Alert. Focused. He wouldn't kill Caitlyn. Absolutely not. It wasn't in his nature.

Not anymore.

As he thundered toward the hospital with only a few miles left to go, he felt a shattering in his mind, and everything blurred into red. It was at that excruciating moment he knew in his heart of hearts he was going to kill that bitch. Suddenly, he thought he saw the entity standing on the slippery road—or was it an animal—and jammed on the breaks. A squealing sound surrounded him, a slamming impact smashed him, his car soared across the highway, and landed upside down in a water-filled ditch.

CHAPTER 63

CAITLYN STOOD NEXT to Edward and listened to him moan in his sleep.

"Hmph." Cate shook her head.

Will's text warned her that Edward was responsible for a daisy-chain of murders across the Northwest down to Vegas. She had to admit, his skills were impressive. It took intelligence, focus, and organization to have carried off his accomplishments.

But he'd made a mistake that led the cops to him. Which means they'll be digging into her past too. Certainly, they would. It wouldn't be difficult for investigators to pull her employment records and see that she'd worked at several hospitals—maybe a new one every six to eight months—and then she'd moved on. How difficult would it be to put two and two together? It only took one panicky nurse to mentioned the unexplained deaths. How long before the murders linked up to the times and places where she'd worked?

SOMEONE WAS SHAKING his arm. Edward opened his eyes and tried to make out the gauzy image before him.

"They know who you are, asshole. The Copycat Killer."

Cate's face came into focus, but the rest of the room was foggy and gray.

"I've got to say, your work is impressive. I'll bet there are more bodies, right? My dad admitted to more than they found. Thought it would keep him from the death chamber, but it didn't.

"So, ah . . . Why were the paramedics reluctant to rescue the serial killer stuck in a smashed car?" Caitlyn paused, then smiled. "It was murder getting him out." She had a good laugh on that one. "I just made that up." She laughed again.

Edward lifted one arm slightly but dropped it back down.

CHAPTER 64

TIME HAD PASSED. An hour? Two? Maybe more. Lights blinked, and machines beeped. Edward was groggy and uncertain. But one thing he *was* sure of: the hideous entity was sitting on his chest and click-clacking its beak.

"Told you so," The Darkness snapped. "You murdered Psyche and were on your way to kill your ultimate prize." The Darkness clucked. "This was all *you*. Not me. You."

Edward tried to speak but couldn't. His arms and his legs felt loaded with lead, and he ached all over. He watched the entity leap to the top of the IV then heard his room door slide open.

Caitlyn came in like a ghost. At first, he thought the shadow on her shoulder was The Darkness. But his tormentor, still perched on the IV, sharpened its spikes with its beak.

She clicked on the overhead light, and that's when Edward saw the shadow. On Caitlyn's shoulder, along for the ride, was a rat-like beast the size of a rabbit. Brown stain splattered the entity's tiger-shaped teeth, and its yellow eyes stuck out like a tree frog's. Wrapped around Caitlyn's neck, the creature's thorn-covered tail hung like a stole.

"I see you're awake," she said.

Edward moaned in his throat.

"Why did the serial killer die in the hospital?" She grinned then winked. "Because he played chess with the angel of death . . . and lost."

With that, she uncapped the needle on a syringe and held up it up for Edward to see. "A shot of air into the vein is all it takes."

Do it, her entity snorted then glared at Edward.

Edward watched the thrill in her eyes until she shifted her focus away from his face. He felt her hands adjusting the IV needle.

Dear God, please stop her. I don't want to die. It's not my time. Caitlyn!

And then death started its gruesome journey toward Edward's heart. Pain coiled through Edward's muscles. His heartbeat became erratic. Dizziness. Anxiety. Chest pain. His body trembled.

There are cemeteries that are lonely,
graves full of bones that do not make a sound,
the heart moving through a tunnel,
in it darkness, darkness, darkness . . .

"Guess who?" Caitlyn looked proud when she said, "Our favorite. Neruda."
Edward watched Caitlyn inhale the rush of murder—her body stiffened, and her eyes rolled back. The last thing he saw, Cate shuddering her pleasure, and then everything faded to black.

Robbi Sommers Bryant's award-winning books include a novella, 6 novels, 5 short-story collections, and 1 book of poetry. Her work has been published in magazines including *Readers Digest, Redbook, Penthouse*, college textbooks, and many anthologies. As editor-in-chief of the Redwood Writers 2018 anthology, she supervised the creation and publication of *Redemption: Stories From the Edge*. Robbi's work was also optioned twice for television's *Movie of the Week*, and she appeared on TV's *Jane Whitney Show* to discuss her article, "A Victim's Revenge."

Robbi is past president of Redwood Writers, the largest branch of the California Writers Club. Besides writing, her professional focus is developmental editing, content editing, copy editing, and proofreading. She is also a professional writing coach. Find out more at robbibryant.com

CPSIA information can be obtained
at www.ICGtesting.com
Printed in the USA
FSHW010639040321
79084FS

9 781949 290509